# AZURE

## The Silver Series Book 5

### By Cheree L. Alsop

ISBN: 9781477401385
Cover Design by Andy Hair
www.ChereeAlsop.com

To my husband, Michael Alsop,
The best content-editor
A wife could ask for.

To my family for their support,
For their love, and the
Endless adventures.

I love you!

# Chapter 1

I tossed a kernel of popcorn into the air, caught it in my mouth, then a bullet buzzed past my face close enough for me to smell the silver. I fell back in my chair and landed on the red sand with a thud. I rolled to my feet, my heart pounding and eyes searching the darkness. Sounds of a struggle parted the moonless night around the red rocks. I wondered how they found us and what had happened to Riff on night watch, then a shadow rose in front of me and lifted a gun.

I ducked under his arms and barreled him into the stone pillars that rose like sentries through our camp. The huff of air forced from his lungs with the impact sounded loud in the still night as the pillar collapsed behind me. I let him drop to the ground, then punched him in the jaw for good measure. I threw his gun into the darkness and took off to search for my friends.

Brian struggled on the ground with a man who looked to outweigh him by at least a hundred pounds, but he still should have been no match for the werewolf's strength. The scent of warm iron touched my nose and I saw a knife sticking out of Brian's thigh. I grabbed his attacker and hurtled him across the ground where he crashed into the dying remains of our fire. I spared a quick glance for Brian's leg, worried that the knife might be silver.

"I'm fine," he growled between gritted teeth, his hands clamped around the knife to prevent it from doing further damage. "Help the others."

His attacker was rising from the coals and I kicked his arms out from under him as I passed, sending him back into the fire. The sounds of a struggle came from the shadows.

I found Sam just outside the camp with a bullet between his eyes. Loss throbbed through my body and I knelt to check for the thump of his pulse, though my ears told me his heart no longer beat. My teeth clenched in anger and a growl escaped my lips. I couldn't control it any longer. Someone had to pay. I phased into wolf form; my clothes tore away in the haste of the phase, but I didn't care. Black fur ran up my body and settled as the phase completed. I longed for the reassuring touch of moonlight, but my wolf eyes easily made out the rocks and brush of our desert surroundings. I took one last look at Sam, then loped toward the next sounds of battle.

Johnny kicked one man in the stomach and turned to face another, but before he could touch him, I leaped, grabbed the back of the man's neck in my teeth, then turned in the air so my weight and momentum flipped the man backwards into a tree. I ran to the next clearing and tore a chunk out of the leg of a man who was trying to skewer Max with a black bladed knife. He used the distraction to take the knife from the man and slice his throat. Max then phased and followed me to the next struggle.

The other werewolves joined us and we took down our remaining attackers in a smooth, synchronized group as we had practiced so many times with deer and elk. It was easy to pretend they were just game instead of humans sent to kill us. To protect my friends, I pulled down human after human and tried to ignore their struggles and protests. They fought back with surprising skill and several werewolves were hurt in the process, but we protected our camp and didn't stop until the threat was gone.

I phased back into human form behind a convenient stand of scrub brush and rocks that also served as a hiding place for one of our many stashes of clothing. I pulled on a set of shorts and rose slowly. The scent of blood tangled with the cinnamon and sun scent of the desert sand. It was a hard battle, but the werewolves were safe. I almost felt the same triumph as when we had a successful hunt, but the taste of blood lingered in my mouth and the sharpness of it reminded me that we hadn't survived easily.

I avoided looking at the faces of the fallen men and focused on my injured comrades. Johnny was hunched next to a tree, his arm sliced to the bone and a bruise forming around one eye, but he shook off my efforts to help, insisting that others needed it worse.

I could barely look at Sam's body; a pang of guilt tore through me. I should have known they were coming. I should have protected him. I took a steeling breath and walked back to camp. Several of my group had gathered around three men, two of whom shouted insults and threats. My head throbbed from a blow I had taken during the heat of the fight. I rubbed my eyes.

"Shut them up," I growled.

"They say there's more coming," Zach, a gray, said over his shoulder.

"They would have been here already," I replied. "It wouldn't make sense for them to attack at separate times." I gave the loudest man a piercing stare. "Isn't that right?"

He sputtered for a second, then replied, "You're wrong. They're on their way and you're gonna die like the filthy beasts you are."

"We aren't the ones who came into your home and killed your friends and family for no reason," I barked out with an edge of anger. Sam's death and the attack threatened to break my control in the face of a man who so openly defied me.

"No reason?" The man let out a snort of disbelief. "You're an abomination and every one of you deserves to die. The Hunters won't stop until every man, woman, and child werewolf is wiped from this earth."

I gritted my teeth against a retort and tipped my head at Max who stood behind him. Max nodded and he and Zach dragged them from the camp. I glanced at the last captive and my heart slowed.

The Hunter was a girl close to my age. She struggled between Drake and Seth, fighting to hold a knife that Seth tried to pry from her hands. Her eyes met mine and I was surprised by her irises, a bright green the color of spring grass after a rain. Her eyes were clouded with pain, but held a spark of defiance despite the odds she faced. She knew she was defeated, but she didn't give up. My heart went out to her. Against reason, I took a step forward.

"Let her go."

Drake and Seth stared at me like I had gone mad. Drake, a gray who always listened to his superiors, let go of her and stepped back, but Seth kept a tight hold on her arm. "She's a Hunter," he protested.

I fought back a growl at his defiance and attributed it to adrenaline from the attack. I met his eyes and glared until he dropped his gaze and let the girl go. She fell to her knees in the dirt, blood pouring from a long, narrow gash in her leg and a scrape above her eye. I wondered how many other wounds her dark clothing hid.

"What's going on here?" Brian demanded. He limped into the clearing with Ben's help. The brothers looked from me to the girl and I stepped between them to shield her.

"She's been hurt enough," I said. I met their eyes, my heart pounding and an edge of recklessness to my thoughts.

Both Alphas looked like they wanted to argue, but Brian wasn't in any shape to fight and Ben wouldn't put his brother in danger. The Alphas knew they would lose if they tried to defy me on even ground, let alone with one of them hurt. My strength and size was the only thing that kept the balance at Two. Ben was about to say something, then he glanced behind me and his eyes widened.

Before I could move, something sliced across my back. I

turned and stared at the girl in amazement. She stood holding the bleeding gash across her thigh, the knife in her hand and her chest heaving. Her long black hair tangled around her face. My teeth lifted back in a snarl at the feeling of blood running down my back. I fought down the urge to slap her. "Don't do that again if you value your life," I said in a growl.

She opened her mouth to reply, then her face paled and her eyes rolled back. She fell forward and I caught her before she hit the ground. The knife fell with a tiny thump to the sand. I lifted her up and her head lolled against my chest. She felt tiny in my arms.

I turned to the other werewolves and Brian smirked at me. "Good luck with that," he said. Ben helped him inside and the other werewolves followed close behind. I glanced around at the destruction of our camp, stone columns riddled by bullet holes, chairs upturned, and the fire scattered with the coals burning out. The sharp scent of blood covered the normal sandy cinnamon and sage smell of the night air. The girl moaned in my arms. I hesitated at the mouth of Two, then ducked through the entrance. I ignored the stares of the other werewolves as I made my way to my quarters.

The red rock walls and caverns that made up our home held the scent of the many werewolves I lived with. The floor had been laid with marble, but the thin red dust that coated everything from the sandstone walls made the surface slippery in the best of times. Brian and Ben had slacked off on sweeping lately and it wasn't worth the fight to keep them working.

Starlight from the thick glass above filtered down to create snake-like patterns on the rocks and marble. I turned at the fork and followed the left branch past the cavern that made up the dining area and kitchen. I took a shortcut through the empty workout room and stopped in front of my door at the back corner of Two. It was solitary and secure, just the way I liked it.

I turned the handle and pushed the door open with my shoulder. Less light streamed through the glass along the ceiling because we were deeper down, but I liked the cool air and the solitude was welcome after the numerous fights that inevitably broke out among the group. Two's position as a haven for hideaway male werewolves definitely came with a price.

My feet sunk into the thick carpets when I crossed to set the girl on my couch. A small sound escaped her lips. I folded my arms and watched her. She looked small on the couch, younger than my nineteen years, but not by much. I wondered if it was bravery or foolishness that gave her the fire to stand up to a dozen werewolves alone. I shook my head and went back out the door to find our resident doctor in training.

\*\*\*

"Tie it off there."

I followed Traer's directions and tied the bandage together at the front of the girl's thigh. He had already completed the stitches and was focused on a nasty looking bite on her forearm.

He wiped his forehead with his sleeve and pushed his glasses further up his nose. "Permission to be frank?"

I rolled my eyes and dipped a cloth in the bowl to clean a deep scrape along her other arm. "You're my friend. Say what you want."

He glanced at me, then concentrated on stitching the gashes back together. "Why save her? There are over a dozen dead Hunters out there and four werewolves. She's one of the enemy."

I didn't answer for a few minutes. I had already asked myself the same question, knowing I would be held accountable as soon as my mother called, but I couldn't explain why I felt so strongly about not letting her die with the rest of them. I felt Traer's eyes on me and shrugged. "I don't know. Look at her."

He stopped stitching and studied her for a minute. "Well, she's young, quite pretty, and a trained killer. Quick with a knife, too, I hear." He tipped his head toward my back meaningfully.

I shook my head. "If she was trained, she would have stabbed instead of sliced."

Traer's eyebrows rose. "You're sidestepping the fact that she cut you with her knife and you still defended her against Ben and Brian. A dangerous move, I might add."

I tossed the bloody cloth onto the counter and picked up some gauze. "They'll live, and they know better than to mess with me."

He nodded. "For now. Your size will only protect you for so long. One of these days they're going to attack when you're weak." I rolled my eyes at the words he had said many times before. Two was still mine and their strength was no match against me. His brow creased. "You didn't answer my question."

We both knew I didn't have to answer anything to a gray, but he was my friend and had never been anything but true to me. I wiped the blood from my hands with a clean cloth and shrugged. "She looked like she needed help."

"She's not some injured puppy, Vance." He glanced at me. "You can't keep a Hunter here without consequences. Too many lives are at stake."

"Tell me about it," I said quietly. I threw my rag with the others. "Would you rather I had let her die?"

Traer didn't reply. He tied off his last stitch, wrapped a bandage around her arm with smooth, deft movements, and checked the other bandages one last time. He sighed. "Well, she might live. She lost a lot of blood and the grays definitely gave her a working over, but she's still breathing so we'll see if she lasts the night. Humans heal a lot slower. A wound we'd recover from in a day could kill them by infection before it's even had a chance to close."

I frowned down at her still form. "Tell me something I don't know."

Traer glanced at me. "You're going to have to explain this to your parents?"

My lips twisted into a wry smile. "No doubt Ben's already beat me to the punch. You'd think they were his parents the way he fills them in on everything that happens here."

"And twists it to fit a profitable point of view?"

"Exactly." I let out a breath. "I'll deal with them tonight when they call. For now, help the others clean up and give me an account of the injured and dead." I rubbed my knuckles absently and a thought occurred to me. "Traer?" He turned at the door. "Have the boys bring what weapons they collect. The scent of silver in the bullets was stronger. We need to see what they're using."

He nodded and pulled the door shut behind him. I stretched gingerly. My shirt clung to the knife wound along my back, but it was already healing and was nothing more than an annoyance. I sat slowly on a chair by the fireplace and studied the still form of the girl.

Straight black hair swept across the side of her face in a soft caress, accentuating fair skin and full lips. Her brow creased as though she felt pain, but Traer said that his sedative wouldn't wear off for hours. I stood up again. It was too much to be in a room with a Hunter while my comrades were gathering bodies and tending to the wounded. I went to the door, then paused at the question of if she would be safe while I was gone. A small smile touched my lips at my foolishness. If there was anything a werewolf respected, it was territory. She would be fine as long as she stayed in my quarters.

I shut the door behind me and walked down the hallway, trailing my hand along the red rock walls in a habit that had stayed with me since childhood. The familiar rough grains under my fingertips calmed my troubled thoughts. I followed the twists and turns of the natural rock formations to the wide dining room. Natural benches carved from the red rocks were interspersed with worn couches, a television set that had seen better days, and a dining table that had once been my mother's newest fad, but now showed the dents, scratches, and carvings of fourteen werewolves stuck in one place for too long.

Thomas was there, the other Alpha besides myself and the Lopez brothers. He tended to Johnny's arm and glanced up to meet my eyes when I walked in. His expression was a mixture of concern and amusement. "Found a pet?"

"Very funny," I replied.

Zach came in with Max close behind.

"What's the report?" I asked.

Zach cleared his throat. "Riff, Sam, Jason, and Sy are dead."

I took a slow breath to ease the anger that ran through my veins. The urge to hit something flared and I rubbed my knuckles. Several of the werewolves closest to me backed up and dropped their eyes.

Ben continued, "Johnny, Drake, and Brian were wounded but recovering. Twenty-four Hunters are dead."

I stared at him. "Twenty-four? What'd they do, bring a small army?"

"Looks like it." He met my eyes, his gaze serious. "They were definitely out for blood."

Ben walked into the room. "I put the guns on your table. That Hunter's sleeping on your couch." He gave me an accusing look.

The hair on the back of my neck stood up and I fought to keep my tone calm. "What do you want me to do, have her sleep on the floor?"

"If she has to sleep anywhere," he said.

My control slipped. "She's not an animal," I snapped before I could stop myself.

"Neither are we," he growled back. "Yet they hunt us like vermin."

"And I did my share to stop them," I said in a tone that warned he was about to step over the edge.

Zach cleared his throat, his eyes on the ground. "By my count, Vance killed fourteen of the Hunters himself."

Ben's eyes widened in surprise, then narrowed. "Why keep the girl then? She's one of them."

"That's what they say about us," I pointed out. "She was

obviously inexperienced and I didn't feel like she deserved to die."

"Did Sam?" Ben asked softly.

I leaped at him and it took four werewolves to hold me back. Larger than any of them, I often felt more like a bear than a wolf. I waited until I felt under control again, then shrugged them off. The knife wound across my back had open again and start to bleed. I rubbed my forehead and sighed. "Zach, Max, take the trucks and haul the Hunters' bodies to White Horse Canyon." I met Ben's eyes. "We need to prepare our friends' bodies to send home to their families."

He looked like he wanted to say something, then he nodded and turned away. I sat next to Johnny. "How's the arm?"

He grimaced when Thomas touched a particularly painful area. "Just peachy," he said from between gritted teeth.

I gave a small smile. "What's the other guy look like?"

He let out a laugh. "You don't want to know."

Traer entered the room with his physician bag. He tended to Johnny's arm in silence, stitching the wound with just enough thread to hold it together so it would heal without scarring. He then nodded toward my back. "You gonna let me take care of that?"

"It's fine." I shrugged, then winced. It should have started healing, which meant the knife she had used was silver and there were possibly fragments in the wound. I gave up and pulled my shirt off, then leaned forward in my chair.

"By fine, you mean still bleeding and full of silver slivers?" Traer replied, frowning. He pulled instruments from his bag and got to work.

# Chapter 2

I met Ben and Thomas in the storage room. The bodies of our friends had been laid gently on the tables we usually used to clean our weapons. It felt wrong to smell their blood mixed with the tang of steel and oil. Sam's pale face stared unseeing at the recessed lights above. The life was gone from his gaze. It was as though I looked into the vacant eyes of a fallen elk. I reached out and closed his eyelids with a hand that covered up most of his face. His cool skin sent a rush of regret through my body and I fought down the urge to phase and run away, leaving the others to do the job I dreaded.

I dressed Sam in the clothes he saved to wear when his parents came to visit. The black shirt, red tie, and slacks failed to hide the haunting wound in his forehead that glared at the edge of my vision no matter where I looked. I combed his hair, smoothing down the cowlick that persisted stubbornly in front. His black hair stuck up again despite my efforts and I blinked back tears at memories of him running through Two, his eyes bright and hair a mess as he followed me around. Three years younger than me, the kid was constantly into everything to show me he was old enough to be my second despite the lack of the usual hierarchy of a pack within Two. I turned away with the painful thought that I wouldn't hear his footsteps trailing me any longer.

Ben and Thomas finished with the other bodies, and then as if on cue the remaining werewolves in our group filed into the room. It felt small, cramped with the scent of werewolves and blood, steel and pain. No one spoke and eyes flitted over the bodies to rest on me, waiting.

I dreaded the words I had never spoken, words that were inevitable now. I took a breath, let it out, then said quietly, "My brothers, bodies of flesh and blood no longer your souls hold. Run without the confines of bone and sinew, howl without the constriction of lungs or breath, and live within the embrace of the moon and her welcoming light. Your lives are one with wolvenkind, and your hearts will beat with ours forevermore. You will not be forgotten."

The other werewolves repeated the words four times, once for each slain brother, in a low chant that echoed mine. The voices spoke the words that had been passed on to us by our parents and drilled into our thoughts when we were young. The words were older than our parents' parents. Each werewolf at Two knew the chant, but none had ever wished to repeat it. It felt final, as though as the last word faded away it took the souls of the werewolves with it.

I closed my eyes and a howl reverberated from my chest. I never howled in human form, but the Uniting Chant required it, combining both the human words with the mourning cry of the wolf. A wolf howl expressed pain and sorrow far above the limited words of the human, and I put every throb of pain and loss from my heart into the howl. The others waited until my voice rose, then theirs lifted as well to mingle heavy and full of sorrow in the room. When I stopped, the tones echoed down the long red rock corridors, whispering back to us as though the souls of those who had been slain called in answer, their voices faint from the life beyond.

I set a hand on Sam's head and closed my eyes again. "Never forgotten, always one," I whispered. I moved to Sy's table and did the same. The others followed me, their voices quiet after the howl. When I finished with Jason and Riff, I left the room and walked down the corridor to one of the back exits we rarely used. The footsteps of the others faded away behind me. The ritual was done, now everyone would have their space to mourn alone.

Once my feet touched the sand still warm from the sun, I took off my shirt and phased. I padded away from Two, my mind escaping into the simpler thoughts of the wolf. The loss pounded with every beat of my heart, and the thought that I had failed those who looked to me for protection echoed over and over in my head. I bowed my head and let me paws take me away from Two and the sorrow that would meet me when I returned.

***

I walked back to my room later that evening, my mind heavy with loss. I kept seeing Sam's blue eyes, open but blank to the world, no reflection of life left where such a spark of joy and excitement had been. I put my forehead against the door to my quarters for a minute; the cool metal brought a slight relief to my pounding headache. I pushed the door open, shut it behind me, then was blinded by a spark and something slammed into my shoulder. It took me a second for my eyes to clear so I could make out the Hunter girl crouched beside my couch with a gun in her hand.

"Are you crazy?" I demanded. I gestured toward the door. "I'm the only thing standing between you getting torn to pieces by a dozen angry werewolves."

She glanced uncertainly at her gun, then glared at me. "Don't you feel pain? Shouldn't you be dead on the floor or something?"

I fought back a growl and took a step toward her. "I'm concentrating on not tearing you apart myself right now."

"Like an animal," she said with a satisfied tone as if I had answered a question she hadn't voiced.

"Like someone who just got shot." I crossed the space between us and ripped the gun from her hands, then threw it across the room. "If you recall, you attacked us. We were minding our own business when you came to camp with guns blazing."

"You're werewolves," she said as if that should answer it.

"We bleed just like you," I shot back.

Footsteps ran down the hall followed by pounding on the door. "Vance, you alright?"

I glared at the girl and she cowered against the couch. I made my way back to the door and leaned against it, my shoulder on fire. "Everything's alright. I was just testing out these new guns."

Thomas' voice was doubtful. "Try it outside next time. It'll keep you from going deaf."

"I'll keep that in mind," I replied dryly.

He waited for a minute outside the door, then his footsteps receded down the hall.

My arm tingled and fingers were numb. I flexed them and turned back to the girl. "What did you guys add to these bullets, anyway?"

Her face was pale as if she realized I had just saved her life again. I didn't have any doubts as to what Thomas would do if he found out she had shot me. She swallowed. "Uh, I'm not sure. My dad's the one who makes them."

The numbness was spreading up my arm to my chest and throat. It started getting harder to breathe. I made my way to the kitchen and fumbled through the drawers for anything I could use. I found tongs, a sharp knife, and a bottle of rubbing alcohol, then sat down at the table still laden with guns. I was careful to face the girl in case she tried anything.

I gingerly took off my shirt and tossed it to the floor. The girl's breath caught at the sight of the wound. I met her eyes and was taken back again by how bright green they were. She held my gaze, her expression unreadable. "You going to take out the bullet by yourself?" she asked; my ears caught a slight tremble to her voice.

I shrugged, then winced. "You see anyone else here?" I dumped some rubbing alcohol on a rag, then used it to the clean the knife and tongs. I glanced at my shoulder. Angry red lines streaked away from the wound. I hesitated, then poured rubbing alcohol on it as well. My shoulder throbbed at the burn. I slammed the bottle back down and held the edge of the table. My vision blurred and it took several minutes for it to clear.

"You okay?" the girl asked, a worried edge to her voice

I forced myself to stay upright. "Whatever your dad coated around these bullets is strong. Tell him kudos for that." I touched the wound. The edges were hot and angry and hadn't started to close. I picked up the tongs, fought down the urge to throw up, and stuck it in the wound. I breathed through my nose to keep from passing out at the pain. White streaks danced in front of my vision.

The girl walked toward me. I stood up to defend myself, then my legs gave out and I fell to the floor. The jolt sent the tongs deeper into my shoulder and I bit back a yell.

"I'm trying to help you," the girl said, her voice anxious. Her hands were soft and tiny over mine. She kept one hand on my chest and took the tongs in the other. Fire raced through my body as she worked to pull out the bullet. She breathed softly, her face inches from mine and her eyes tight with concentration.

"Almost got it," she whispered to herself.

A spasm shook my body. She grabbed the bullet with the tongs and pulled it free, then held me down the best she could and poured more rubbing alcohol into the wound. The burn of the liquid slowly stole through my body and chased away the paralyzing effects of the bullet's coating. My labored breathing eased and vision slowly came back into focus. I squinted and made out the girl crouched over me, her eyes wide with concern and fear.

"Did I kill you?" she whispered.

I nodded and a tight smile touched the corners of her lips. "That's what you get for saving me," she said softly.

I rested my head back against the cold tile floor and took several deep, calming breaths. The pain of the wound was already fading and I could think again. I eased myself up so that my back rested against the oven.

"I don't think you should move," the girl protested.

"I'm just glad I can," I replied. I flexed my hand, relieved to find that the numbness was almost gone. I set my head back and concentrated on breathing.

"Are any other werewolves as big as you?" she asked quietly.

I fought back a small smile. "Not that I've met," I replied with my eyes closed, "But that number is limited." I let out a breath and tipped my head to look at the girl. "Your Hunters killed four of my friends today."

The sadness that swept across her face was genuine. She dropped her eyes and nodded. "I know. We were just scouting. They weren't supposed to attack, but Jerome's always itching to kill."

"Do others know you're here?" I studied her face, looking for any sign that she would lie to me.

She closed her eyes and shook her head. "We weren't even supposed to be this far south. Rumor had it that a werewolf was spotted at a town about twenty miles north. We didn't find any sign and kept going. We practically ran into your sentry."

The tracks and Riff's unfired flare gun told the same story. It took a lot to ambush an Alpha. I wondered if he had fallen asleep from his late night with Marcie. I rubbed my eyes with my right hand. I shouldn't have let him keep his scheduled watch, but he insisted and sometimes it was easier to give in than to argue. Arguing Alphas wasn't a pretty sight, and Two had taken more than its fair share of brawling. Now he was dead.

"What about the other Hunters?" the girl asked softly, dread in her voice.

I didn't know how to soften the blow. I let out a slow breath. "They're all dead."

She leaned against the table with her eyes closed. A tear leaked from between her lashes and rolled down her cheek.

"Were they your friends?"

She nodded. "Most of them. They were Hunters in training. I wasn't supposed to go out with them, but Jerome convinced me." She turned her head and met my eyes, her own heavy with sorrow. "I shouldn't have gone."

I took a deep breath and winced when it pulled at my shoulder. "I know I'd be in better shape."

Her eyes took on a brief glimpse of humor that was quickly chased away by sorrow. She pushed up from the ground, then stumbled on her injured leg. I caught her before she could fall, biting my teeth against the pain that jolted through my shoulder. I noticed for the first time that blood had soaked through the bandage on her thigh.

"You should be resting," I rebuked gently.

"I will if you will," she replied in a weary voice.

I glanced at the guns on the table. "Do I need to hide these first?"

A pained smile touched her lips. "I promise I won't shoot you again."

"And the other werewolves?"

She nodded.

"And no more slicing people?"

She rolled her eyes and stood slowly. I rose next to her, fighting back a smile when she tried to help. "Not so big and bad, right?"

She didn't answer and limped toward the couch. I shook my head. "You take the bed. I won't be sleeping much tonight anyway."

She looked like she wanted to argue, but weariness reflected in her expression; she nodded wordlessly before heading toward the bedroom. I followed her, grabbing some clean bandages from the table on my way past. She glanced back at me with a guarded expression. I lifted the bandages and she sat on the edge of the bed.

23

Traer had cut her pants high enough to tend to the thigh wound. The girl pulled the cloth back and let me wrap another set of bandages around her leg. Her face was white, her green eyes and black hair a sharp contrast to her pale skin. Dark circles had begun around her eyes. She watched me quietly with unreadable thoughts hiding behind her searching gaze.

"You need to sleep," I said. I helped her back on the bed and put a light blanket over her.

"I feel bad taking your bed," she said softly.

"I hear roughing it on the couch is good for character," I replied. I went to the door and watched her for a minute in case she needed anything, but her soft, steady breathing said that she was already asleep. She looked so small in the bed my mother had specially ordered to fit my hulking size.

I turned away at the thought that she was a Hunter who had come to kill my friends. She might not have been the instigator, but I had no way of knowing if any of the deaths I mourned had been at her hand. I settled on the couch, weary and with a throbbing shoulder. I glanced back once at the bedroom, then rose and shut the door. The sound of it opening should awaken me if I didn't sleep too deeply.

I sat back on the couch and leaned my head on the cushion. The scent of my parents had long since vanished from its fabric, and only the smell of the girl tangled with my scent that colored everything in my room. No one else came in here. The thought comforted me and brought bitterness at the same time. I rolled over and gave in to the dark shadow of sleep.

# Chapter 3

I awoke to the sound of running water. It took me a minute to remember where I was and why my shoulder throbbed with each beat of my heart. I pushed up from the couch gingerly and followed the sound to the bathroom. The door was open a crack and the scent of water drifted out. I put a hand on the doorknob to pull it shut and give the girl some privacy, but the mirror showed her huddled on the floor of the shower, her arms around her knees, her head bowed, and her clothes still on. My heart slowed at the scent of blood and the memory of her injuries.

"Are you okay?" I asked just loud enough to be heard over the shower.

When she didn't answer, I stepped inside. I crossed the bathroom and pulled open the clear plastic shower door. She didn't look up at me, her head on her knees despite the pain it must cause to her thigh. I reached down slowly and touched the top of her head. The water that soaked it was freezing.

"What are you trying to do, die of hypothermia?" I asked. I adjusted the water so that it was warm, but she didn't move. I took a steeling breath and, for lack of other options, eased myself slowly down beside her. I felt like a giant next to her tiny, graceful form. I didn't know what to do with my arms, so settled for crossing them in front of my chest. My shoulder ached, but I ignored it.

Several minutes passed in an empty silence. I didn't know what to do. She was a Hunter and her friends had killed mine. My parents would demand that I execute her, yet she looked so small and pitiful sitting on the floor of the shower. The sorrow in her eyes reflected the ache in my heart. The silence lengthened, broken only by the patter of water against the tile. She then turned her head to look at me, her eyes red along with her cheeks and nose. "All my friends are dead." Water dripped down her face, adding to the miserable sadness I read there.

I swallowed against the knot that formed in my throat. "Mine, too." I lifted my good arm and she ducked under it. She shivered against my side and I held her close until the warm water chased away her chills. Her muscles relaxed and I felt her lean into me. I tipped my cheek against the top of her head and felt the soft brush of her hair against my chin. We stared off together in silence, no longer alone in our pain. The minutes stretched until time didn't matter; all that mattered was that my enemy needed me, and I needed her, too.

\*\*\*

Her breathing slowed and it eventually turned to the steady rhythm of sleep. I reached up and turned off the shower with one hand while keeping her in place with the other. I fumbled for the towel hanging on the outside of the shower door, then wrapped it around her the best that I could. I knelt and gathered her in my arms, afraid that I would hurt her with any quick movements. I pushed open the shower door with my foot and made my way quietly down the hall.

I hesitated at the bed. The blankets were rumpled and I didn't know if she would prefer to be above or beneath them wearing wet clothes. She shivered in my arms and I opted for beneath. I pulled them back with a free finger, then slid her underneath and tucked them around her body. Her face looked pale with her long black hair splayed wetly around her. I put one last blanket above her feet and turned to go, then she said something so softly I couldn't make it out.

My heart gave a strange sideways thump and I knelt quietly next to the bed so I wouldn't wake her if she was talking in her sleep. Her eyelids fluttered, but her eyes didn't open. "Would you stay with me?" she repeated. Her voice was so small and forlorn I had to swallow past a lump that rose in my throat.

After all she had been through, I couldn't deny her anything. My heart pounding, I walked quietly around to the other side of the bed feeling more like a lurching bear than I ever had before. I climbed as gently as I could on top of the blankets and lay down about a foot from her. I lifted my arm awkwardly, wondering where I should put it, then she turned without a word and burrowed against my side with her hands tucked under her chin. I hesitated, then lowered my arm slowly so that it rested along the outside of her body. She gave a small sigh that sounded like a sob, then her breathing grew steady once more.

I lay in my bed with a girl sleeping against my side. I had never touched a girl, let alone had one in my bed. I told myself that it didn't matter, she was a Hunter and would no doubt hate me in the morning; but with the midnight stars winking down through the glass ceiling above and the cinnamon scent of the red rocks mixing with her feminine vanilla and sunflower aroma, it did matter. For the first time in my life, someone truly needed me.

My heart lurched at the thought. At Two I told myself I was needed, that the werewolves would fall apart and not know what to do with themselves if I wasn't around, but we were older now and most were ready to begin their own lives. My parents had long ago made it clear I wasn't a pivotal part of their existence. No one had ever looked at me with need and loss so bright in their eyes.

The Hunter's heart beat against mine and I closed my eyes, but sleep was the furthest thing from my mind. My heart raced and I reminded myself that it was alright. I wouldn't hurt her. I would keep her safe. I had never been so close to a woman. Her scent filled my nose, strange and female, an aroma of flowers amid the musk and brawn of the male werewolves who inhabited Two. My muscles were tight and my arms strained not to hurt her. It would take a mere flick of my wrist to snap her neck. The thought scared me and I wondered why she wasn't more afraid.

I was a good guy. I kept telling myself that over and over. I saw in my mind's eye the image of me pulling down her Hunter friends one after the other. I tried to remember that they had come to kill us first, but with her huddled beneath my arm in pain because of their deaths, it was hard to keep things in perspective. Guilt filled me as I watched her breathe, her face serene in sleep. I wondered how she could trust me enough to rest beside me after all I had done.

Her eyebrows pulled together as I watched, a look of pain crossing her face. I hesitated, then touched her cheek softly with the back of my fingers. Her expression relaxed and she rolled closer against me. My heart pounded in my chest at her nearness. Her black hair drifted across my pillow in a soft wave, her head light on my arm. Sleep eluded me as I watched her, awed by her trust and presence. Hours passed and emotions warred through my mind as I held her.

The golden light of dawn filtered through the thick glass of the ceiling by the time she stirred. I hadn't moved a muscle, the sound of her breathing and the beat of her heart enough to keep me perfectly still so I wouldn't awaken her. I told myself I was foolish. She had fallen into a deep sleep long ago and wouldn't have noticed if the roof fell in on her. I wondered if my presence had helped her sleep so well, then told myself that it was her injury and the stress she had been through.

I watched the way the morning light brushed across the curve of her cheek. She was beautiful and graceful, tiny like a dancer but strong willed and ferocious when she needed to be. Her presence set my whole world on a tilt, but I would do it again without hesitation. Her breathing changed and her eyes opened slowly to stare into mine. The regret and anger I expected to see in them never appeared; instead, she watched me in silence and her hand rested on my arm, a simple touch that said so much more than words ever could.

# Chapter 4

My cell phone rang a few hours later while I rested in a daze on the couch. The screen said it was my mother and I let out a breath in a slow whoosh. I sat up slowly, closed my eyes, and opened the phone. I pushed the speaker button and set it on the arm of the couch by habit.

"Vance, what on earth is going on over there?" Mom demanded in her usual get-to-the-point way. "Ben told us about the attack, the boys who were killed, and you have a Hunter in your apartment? What on earth are you thinking? You need to kill her right now."

"Hello to you, too, Mom," I replied dryly. I could practically feel her wanting to strangle me over the phone and fought back a small, sad smile. "It's been an eventful night."

"Ben said we lost Sam."

"And Riff, Jason, and Sy," I said. My heart slowed with each name.

Mom let out small breath. "How did they find you?"

"By accident. No one else knows we're here."

"Except the Hunter in your apartment." I knew by her tone that her hands were clenched into fists and she had her jaw set in the way that always stopped me in my tracks as a child. I was grateful I no longer spoke to her through the computer where I could see her.

"We can learn from her," I said carefully.

"About what, how to kill werewolves?" Mom asked.

I rolled my eyes and hunched down further on the couch. I winced when the motion pulled at my healing shoulder and sat back up. "I'll be careful. I need to go help Thomas and Ben with the coffins."

Mom's voice came softer, "Did you perform the Uniting Chant?"

"For each of them," I replied. It felt as though a vice

gripped my heart. I shut my eyes tightly, willing the emotions to stay locked deep inside.

Mom fell silent for a moment, then she said with a tight voice, "I called Sam's mom." My heart ached and I heard the quiet sniff that said she was crying but didn't want me to know.

I asked quietly, "How did she take it?"

Mom sniffed again. "Not well. She was mad, then heartbroken. She's trying to gather the others to seek revenge."

"We killed them." My stomach turned at the words, but I kept my voice expressionless.

"She wants to go after their parents." Anger laced through her tone. "I don't blame her, Vance. I would do the same. It sounds like it was a close thing."

"It was," I admitted. "I never thought they'd get this far."

"We're going to have to make some changes at Two."

I nodded even though she couldn't see me. She took the silence for agreement, told me she loved me, and hung up the phone with the promise to call tomorrow and make sure preparations were taking place.

I closed the phone, then rested my elbows on my knees and buried my face in my hands. The images of my dead friends' faces danced in my mind, their wounds bleeding and eyes lifeless. Tears rose unbidden and slid between my fingers.

"Your mom sounds like a piece of work," a voice said from behind me.

My fingers found the knife hidden under the cushion and I spun with the blade out to stop a millimeter from the girl's throat. My heart raced and it took a minute to slow my breathing and force the urge to phase back down. The Hunter's wide eyes stared into mine, bright with fear and surprise. I lowered the knife.

"Don't you know better than to startle an armed werewolf?"

"I didn't know you were armed," she said in a strangled voice.

I slid the knife back under the cushion, my eyes never leaving her face. "Always assume I'm armed."

"I will."

I couldn't tell if she was serious or mocking me, so I kept silent.

Her eyes searched my face. "Oh, you're crying," she said in a tone that was surprised and tender the way someone would talk to a lost puppy.

She put a hand on my shoulder. The gesture was so familiar and sweet I didn't know how to respond. No one ever touched me, let alone in consolation. Crying and being comforted was a weakness I couldn't afford. I gritted my teeth and moved away from her hand. "Your Hunters killed my friends. Now I have to send their bodies home to their families."

She shook her head with regret shining in her green eyes. "They should be alive. We weren't supposed to be here. It was a mistake."

"One that cost all of us dearly," I replied softly, thinking of the bodies I had prepared and the quiet, mournful tones of the Uniting Chant. The thought sent a sharp pain through my heart and I had to change the topic. "What's your name?"

She sniffed, then turned her head to look at me. "Nora."

"I don't think we've been properly introduced," I said, trying for humor. I held out a hand. "I'm Vance."

She looked at my hand until I finally dropped it. Her gaze darkened. "I need to go home."

I shook my head. "I can't let you do that."

"So, what? You'll keep me here forever?"

I bristled at her tone. "At least you're alive. I can't let you endanger the rest of the werewolves by letting you go."

"My dad will come for me," she threatened.

"According to you, he has no idea you're here." I held her eyes, my tone dangerous. "I don't think anyone's coming."

She glared at me for a moment, making me realize that it had been years since anyone had met my gaze with so much defiance. I rose and crossed to the door. "Better get some more rest," I said over my shoulder. "You need to give your leg a chance to heal."

I shut the door and stalked down the hall angrier than the situation called for. The Hunter confused me. She could be sweet and needy one moment, then prickly as a porcupine the next. She kept me on my toes when all I wanted to do was figure out how to make Two stronger against attacks. I had no doubts that the families of the Hunters we killed would be looking for them, and we had to be ready if they found us.

\*\*\*

I hammered the last few nails on Sam's coffin, then could only sit back and stare at the four wooden boxes. A void filled my chest and it was all I could do to keep from tearing everything apart. With my friends dead, Two possibly compromised, and an unpredictable Hunter in my rooms, there was no peace.

I made my way through the twisted red rock halls to the training rooms. The rooms were empty. I picked up a pair of knives and attacked the first dummy with a smooth efficiency and mindless effort brought by years of practice. I had killed the ten dummies in the room so many times I was almost fond of the wood and cloth forms. I went to the next room and reviewed martial arts with the wooden practice posts. Sweat dripped from my skin and my heart pounded with each hit. My muscles flowed smoothly from one exercise to the next as I had done a million times. I lost myself in the motion. My healing shoulder and back throbbed, but it was a healing ache and I reveled in the pain that crowded the other thoughts from my mind.

"Vance?"

Traer's voice eventually broke through the numb fog of battle exhaustion that chased away all thoughts but my pretend opponents. I gave him a weary smile and tossed the pair of sticks I had been using back in a pile.

Traer's eyes tightened with concern. "What happened there?"

I glanced down at my chest and saw that the strain of practice made the bullet wound start bleeding again. My white shirt had a big red tell-tale circle along the front of my left shoulder. I met my friend's eyes. "Just a scratch from the fight, that's all."

He lifted an eyebrow. "It should have started healing by

now." His expression said he suspected something different.

I held his eyes. "If I say it's a scratch, it's a scratch."

He hesitated, then lowered his eyes to the ground and nodded. "Very well. We need to check the Hunter's wounds and probably change the bandages."

"Fine."

He led the way from the room, my Alpha instincts more comfortable with following instead of having someone at my back. Even all the years we had lived together couldn't dampen the survival instincts.

# Chapter 5

"How does this feel?" Traer asked in an emotionless tone.

"Could you wrap it tighter?" Nora questioned. At Traer's look, she blushed slightly. "It would help me get around better if I wasn't worried about pulling the stitches."

Traer glanced at me and at my nod unwound the bandages and started over. His deft fingers made a mockery of the wrapping job I was doing on her arm. When he finished, he glanced at my work, sighed, and rewrapped that one, too.

I leaned back against the kitchen counter and crossed my arms over my chest. The position helped ease the healing throb from my shoulder. Nora watched Traer work, an unreadable expression on her face. I couldn't tell if she was afraid of the werewolf or surprised by his knowledge of medicine. She gave a small cough and I realized I was staring.

"I noticed the degrees in the bedroom. Are those yours or do you add plagiarizing to your list of werewolf activities along with slaughtering humans like cattle?" she asked with a bite. She winced at Traer's touch that suddenly appeared a bit rougher.

Traer looked at me with a lifted eyebrow. I gave Nora a steady look. "We only slaughter humans like cattle if they come to slaughter us first. Those are the first humans I've ever killed." Shock widened her eyes. I was surprised at how the look hurt, but pushed it aside. "The degrees are mine. We are all schooled online."

"I didn't know you could get a Masters over the Internet."

I met her skeptical gaze directly. "When you have unlimited funds, long-distance schooling isn't an obstacle. Schools will do whatever they can to receive the donations my parents provide. I have a Masters in Ancient Philosophy and English Literature."

"With a Minor in Zoology," she said quietly.

I nodded. "Not much else to do around here but study and slaughter innocents."

She looked abashed at my sarcastic tone and I wanted to take it back, but a knock sounded at the door.

"Vance? Search and Rescue is on the radio. They have hikers lost up Sage Canyon and are requesting our help."

I rubbed the calluses on the palm of my hand and met Traer's expectant expression. The thought of getting out of Two for a while was a welcome distraction. I raised my voice, "Tell Ron we'll be there."

"Will do," Drake replied. His footsteps disappeared back up the hall.

Nora looked from Traer to me. "You've got to be kidding me," she said, her voice thick with disbelief.

"Which part? That hikers are lost or they want our help in finding them?"

I fought back a laugh at Traer's droll tone and met Nora's doubtful gaze. "Believe it or not, werewolves can have a modicum of humanity," I said dryly. I stood up from the counter and went in the bedroom to change my shirt and grab hiking boots, a compass, and a map. The last two items were purely for show, but appearances were everything when it came to hiding what we really were.

I went back into the living room to find Nora and Traer arguing.

"I just don't think it'd be a good idea. They know us and they don't know you. We don't have any reason for you to come along on something like this," Traer said. His back was to me, but I could tell by the tension in his shoulders that he was annoyed.

"I could help," Nora pointed out.

Traer's voice was deep with sarcasm. "By limping up a

trail and tearing your stitches?" He paused. "Of course, if you bleed out it really would be helpful."

Hurt swept through her eyes, but it was replaced by defiance. "For your information, I grew up in the canyon lands and I've helped on my fair share of hikes. An extra pair of eyes won't hurt."

He gave a slight laugh. "It's not eyes we need. We've got it covered."

"I don't think it'd hurt if she came," I said quietly from the doorway. The thought of leaving her alone with the other werewolves wasn't a pleasant one. The chance of the Alphas entering my room didn't seem a long stretch after what we had been through.

Traer turned, protest on his face. "She'd slow us down."

"I would not," Nora countered.

"You think you could keep up?" I asked seriously.

"If you can," she shot back, her eyes flashing.

The doctor glanced at her and I saw a brief, reluctant glimmer of humor at her attitude. Our friendship gave him some leeway, but none of the other werewolves dared to talk to me like that.

I shrugged. "You come at your own risk."

"That's how I prefer it," she replied.

Traer rolled his eyes and left. I moved to follow him into the hallway, but she stopped me.

"Uh, Vance?" My heart gave a faint thump at the way she said my name, hesitant, yet familiar.

I turned back slowly. "Yeah?"

"Do you happen to have some pants I could borrow?"

I smiled at the thought of her hiking in her shredded jeans. "I'll find something."

She met us outside a few minutes later in a pair of my sweat pants and a dark blue tee-shirt. Both were too big for her, but she did her best to make them work by rolling the pants at the ankles and waist and tying the shirt on one side. Traer gave a barely stifled sigh of annoyance, and Max and Seth, both in wolf form, avoided looking at her. I motioned for them to jump into the back of the jeep.

"They're going as wolves?" Nora asked, surprised.

"When we find the hikers, we can attribute it to the miraculous tracking of our faithful pets," Traer replied. He climbed into the front passenger seat, leaving Nora to ride in the back next to the wolves. I considered asking him to move, but changed my mind at the stubborn look on her face. Traveling next to phased werewolves might slow her thoughts of escape.

She climbed stiffly into the back and tried to ignore Max and Seth the best that she could. The two gray wolves did the same to her. "When in fact it'll be your tracking skills that find them?" she questioned.

"Vance's. He's the best tracker we've got," Traer replied with a hint of pride.

I climbed into the driver's seat and drove us down the back trail the led away from Two. We took the hour long trip through sandy roads that were little more than dirt trails and ended at the Search and Rescue outpost. Ron, Dave, and several other members we had worked with before met us out front.

"They've been out since Tuesday," Ron said without preamble when I got out of the jeep. The others stayed in their seats to wait for my orders. Ron tipped his hat at them. His eyes lingered on Nora for a split second, then he gave me his usual cheerful smile. "We've had the troop out for the last day and a half, but no good. Either these kids have walked off the face of the earth, or gotten themselves stuck in a crevice somewhere and can't find their way back out."

"How do you know they're missing?"

"The mother of one of the boys called, then came in. She

and several of the other parents are staying at the motel awaiting word." He held up a worn red baseball cap. "She brought this from her son Alex. Think your dogs can track them?"

"Haven't failed us yet," I replied, accepting the cap.

Ron nodded toward a red and yellow jeep. "I'll lead the way."

I climbed back in the driver's seat, took a surreptitious sniff of the cap, then handed it to Traer. He tossed it back to Max and Seth. It landed on Nora's lap and both wolves eyed her warily.

"Oh, it's not like I'm going to bite you," she said crossly before setting it in the seat between them. "I'm the one who should be worried."

Both wolves gave snorts of offense and turned their attention to the hat.

"So how did you get a reputation for Search and Rescue?" Nora asked as we followed the jeep up the road.

Traer smiled without looking back. "Vance found Ron's ten year old daughter out in the Spires when everyone had already written her off as dead. Since then, they call us whenever they have difficult cases."

I glanced at Nora in the rear view mirror and met her searching gaze. Frustrated, but unable to explain why, I turned my attention back to the road and concentrated on the scenery.

We pulled up to a sandy wash about five miles from the station. A green lifted jeep and a beat-up red car sat side by side just off the faint tracks that made up the road. From their tire marks and the sand that coated them, it was obvious they had been there a few days. We climbed out of the jeep and followed Ron and his men to the beginning of the wash. The wolves ran ahead and started sniffing the trail.

"We've searched to the end and expanded half a mile to

each side to no avail. This one's been a challenge," Ron said. He took off his cap and mopped his bald head with a handkerchief before replacing it.

"I like a challenge," I replied.

Nora gave a soft snort of mockery behind me, but I ignored her and glanced at the sun. "No time like the present to find what we're looking for."

"*If* you find something," Ron replied amiably.

I laughed, "*When* we find something."

He chuckled and fell in behind us so they wouldn't mar the tracks any more than they already had.

"What's that about?" Nora asked Traer from my left.

"Ron hates the fact that we can find the hikers they've misplaced," Traer said.

"We don't misplace them," Ron replied from a few paces back. "Hikers are very good at misplacing themselves without our help."

I smiled at his disgruntled tone. "These valleys are full of so many pockets and crevices it takes a team to find them," I replied to soothe his ruffled feathers.

He tipped his baseball hat at me like an old cowboy and turned his attention to Nora. "Glad to meet a new member of Vance's group."

I watched her out of the corner of my eye and fought back a smile when she bristled. "I am not a part of his group."

"Well, uh, a friend then?" Ron pressed, confused at her hostility.

"An acquaintance," she allowed without looking at me. She tripped over a stone and winced.

"Are you alright?" Dave, one of Ron's rescue team, asked quickly.

Nora brushed it off, but her face was pinched with pain. "It's nothing, just sprained my ankle a while back and I'm still working to return it to full strength."

Traer threw me a worried look, but I knew if I sent Nora back to the jeep someone would have to go with her. She was stubborn enough to put up quite a commotion at the suggestion, and I preferred not to deal with that kind of headache while looking for people in a possibly dire situation. Riff's face flashed in my mind and I shied away from the fact that it was the same thinking that might have gotten him killed.

The sun beat down from straight overhead and made waves in the air around us. The trail passed two stone pillars that marked the turn-off for the regular hiking path, then narrowed as we continued down the wash to the point that we had to walk single file with the wolves running ahead. Seth and Max always enjoyed trailing and were usually the werewolves I brought along. They raced ahead, then loped back to encourage us on.

The wolves whined once at several scents that left the wash up a trail to our left, but the smell from the boy's hat wasn't one of them, so I motioned discreetly for the wolves to go on. The pounding in my shoulder faded as my senses sharpened and I focused on the scent of the boy ahead of us mingled with those of his friends. There were at least three different human scents mixed with his that wove in and out of the baked sandy sage aroma of the trail.

Nora started limping slightly, but I pushed on, anxious to reach the group before they had to spend another night in canyons that cooled rapidly after sundown. Traer fell back with her and the Search and Rescue team and the distance slowly increased between us. The wolves trotted silently in front of me, gray tails waving slowly from side to side and fur rippling in a stray spring breeze that made the sand dance like tiny tornadoes in their paw prints. I pressed on after I heard the others take a snack break, reminding myself that as far as we came in, we would have to return and possibly with incapacitated hikers.

We followed the scent down a second wash and I left an arrow of stones to show the others where we had gone. The wolves trotted up the sandy furrow, but I stopped after a few paces. The scent had vanished.

I spun around, testing the air for the guiding scent. When I couldn't find it, I went to the mouth of the wash where it had been, then crouched and studied the landscape carefully. A sandstone wall rose on my right with a slight crack in it. The wash on my left was shallow and had a few boot prints in the bottom, but none of them belonged to the boy's scent. I grabbed a handful of sand and let it flow through my fingers as I looked around.

A broken twig on a sage bush at the top of the wash across from me caught my attention. I rose and dusted off my hands. The ground around the bush looked unbroken, but closer observation showed it to be sandstone that had been swept clear of the top layer of sand that covered everything else. The hard surface wouldn't show footprints.

I crossed the wash and climbed carefully up the other side. The boy's scent covered the bush and a gnarled root he and his friends had used to reach the top. The wolves appeared a moment before I whistled for them. When they climbed the wash next to me and saw where the boy had gone, both Seth and Max looked comically relieved. They ran on ahead and I decided to wait for the others to make sure they didn't miss the trail.

The wolves came back a few seconds later whining and looking anxiously in the direction of the scent. I knew better than to question their judgment. I tore off a strip of cloth from the bottom of my green tee-shirt and tied it to the sage brush, then followed Seth and Max up the trail.

The top of the wash led to a narrow canyon with sheer

walls on either side. My wolf instincts cringed at the thought of being trapped in the enclosed space, but the wolves jogged through as though they had other things to concern them than being cornered. I took a calming breath and followed, my hands trailing on either wall.

The sound was muffled. It was obvious why the Search and Rescue team hadn't been able to find them. The sheer walls and thick sandy floor effectively prevented any yells from reaching the wash where they had turned off. The wolves started running and I jogged after them until they stopped at a hole in the ground that dropped into a red rock cave far below the rim. The hikers started to yell at the sound of our approach.

"Hello? Is anyone up there?"

"Yeah," I shouted down. "I'm Vance. Search and Rescue is close behind."

"Oh, thank goodness," a female voice said. She then shouted, "Don didn't see the hole and fell through. He broke his leg pretty bad. We were climbing down to help him when the rope broke and we got trapped down here."

"How many are there?"

"Four," a male voice called up. "Tina was hurt in the fall, but she says she can climb."

"Just give me a rope long enough get us out of this hole," she replied with a threatening tone that made me smile.

"The others'll be here soon," I promised. I turned to the wolves. "I'm going to climb down and make sure they're alright. Seth, go back to the others and help them find this place without falling in. Max, keep watch in case I need anything."

Both wolves snorted in assent and Seth trotted back down the trail. I studied the hole. Sunlight from high above filtered down through several similar holes to light spots along the floor quite a ways below. I could just make out the hikers under the lip of the cave. It wouldn't be hard to reach them with my werewolf strength. The problem was making it look realistic and I didn't have any rope. I could either wait for the others, or get creative.

Patience wasn't one of my virtues. I lowered myself down the rim, then eased slowly along the wall with my hands and feet on either side.

"What are you doing?" one of the hikers asked in alarm.

I moved down to where the wall suddenly distanced itself, jumped to one side using my hands and feet to slow me, then pushed off to the other side and slid to the bottom. I stood and dusted myself off, then turned to face four surprised stares.

"That was awesome!" one of the boys said. He walked over to meet me with an excited expression on his face. His scent matched the baseball hat, confirming that I had found Alex and his friends.

"Awesomely stupid," the girl who had spoken before replied, her dark eyes flashing. "You didn't bring a rope or anything?"

"I brought this." I tossed her my water bottle. She caught it and gave it to the boy on the ground without looking at me. He took a few thirsty swallows and handed it to the girl next to him. "My team is close behind with ropes, a stretcher, and everything we need to get you out of here. My job is to assess the situation and do what I can before they arrive."

"Don's leg is in bad shape," Alex said. He knelt by his friend and pulled up his pant leg to emphasize. Blood soaked through bandages that had been loosely placed on an open fracture.

I crouched by him and felt for the edges of the break. Don winced but didn't stop me. "The bandages are too loose."

"We didn't want to hurt him," the girl snapped.

I refrained from commenting that blood loss was a lot more dangerous at this point and swiftly unwrapped the bandages. Sharp shards of bone showed stark white through the bleeding tissue. I tossed the dirty rags aside and glanced around for something else to use. There wasn't anything readily available, so I took off my tee-shirt and proceeded to tear it into strips.

I wound the cloth gently but firmly around the open fracture, binding it tight enough to last until we got him back to the Search and Rescue base. Don gripped Alex's hand tightly, but kept silent. I looked up and found him looking at my chest. I glanced down and my stomach turned at the healing bullet wound I had forgotten about. The edges had closed and the skin was a healing pink, but it was obviously from a bullet.

"Where'd you get that?" Don whispered.

I gave a wry smile. "Hunting accident."

His eyes widened, but he nodded. "Looks painful."

"It was," I said with a laugh.

"How'd you get that knife scar?" the girl with the sarcastic tone asked.

I rubbed my eyes and rose. "Same accident, ironically."

"You should probably stop hunting," Alex said with a concerned expression.

I chuckled. "I probably should."

"Is everyone alright down there?" Ron called from above. "Vance, you down there?"

"I'm here," I shouted back. "We have a fractured leg and," I glanced at the bad-tempered girl and the way she favored her foot. "Possibly a sprained ankle." She rolled her eyes, but couldn't hide the pain.

"I'll send Dave down with the harnesses and a splint. I'm getting too old for this stuff."

"You should retire," I called back.

He swore softly and tossed the harnesses down. I caught them and gestured to Alex. "You first."

He shook his head. "Don and Tina are hurt. They should go first."

"We need to secure their injuries before they ascend."

"Then ladies first," he said, gesturing to the other girl.

I nodded. "Fine." I helped her secure the harness and had it ready by the time Dave reached the bottom of the cave. He handed out some nutrition bars and more water to the hikers, then clipped the girl's harness to the rope.

"Ready," he called to the others.

The girl rose slowly, using her feet to walk up the rock face as the team above pulled the rope. She disappeared from view and I helped Alex into the next harness. Dave secured a splint around Don's leg over my bandages, then wrapped it in another set of cloth strips while we waited for the rope to clear.

"Good to go," Ron called down as the rope fell back to the bottom.

Alex rose slowly to the top, his face white and eyes on the sky above the canyon rim.

I took the remaining strips of cloth Dave had brought down and wrapped them around Tina's shoe and ankle while Dave attached her harness.

"Shouldn't I take my shoe off?" she asked dryly.

I shook my head and tied the wrapping tight. "It'll help support your ankle. We have quite a hike back down. The more support you have, the better."

I helped her to her feet and she tested the ankle gingerly. She gave me an approving look. "Definitely better."

I smiled. "You just have to trust me."

I clipped her harness to the rope and watched her walk slowly up the rock. Ron's team tossed down a second rope which Dave used to secure himself so he could rise with the injured boy.

"Ready chief?" Dave asked Don. The boy nodded, his eyes tight. Dave called that they were ready and I helped steady Don as he was lifted into the air. Dave kept him away from the rocks and they rose slowly out of sight.

I glanced around the sandstone cave. The floor was covered in sand so soft it felt like powder between my fingers. I doubted many people had ever been down there. It always felt like a breath of fresh air when I found somewhere few had been, like despite all the chaos and treachery in the world, there were still sacred places left.

"Coming up?" Ron yelled.

I looked back to find the rope tracing patterns in the sand. I glanced around the cave one last time, took a breath of the still air, then slipped into the harness Ron had attached to the rope and walked up the wall.

The first person I saw when I cleared the rim was Nora. She stood with her hands on her hips, her face slightly pale from the strain of the climb and a spark of anger in her green eyes.

"You just jump into a cave with no regard for your safety?" she demanded.

I glanced at Alex and he shrugged apologetically for having told on me.

I sighed. "What? You're concerned about me now?"

She sputtered. "I, well, you have people counting on you and shouldn't be diving headlong into granite caves."

"Sandstone," I corrected with a smile.

She rolled her eyes. "Whatever." Her gaze found the bullet scar on my chest and some of her spark faded. Her eyebrows lowered and she looked like she wanted to say something, then she turned and limped gingerly away.

I pulled off the harness and dusted the red sand off the knees of my pants. Traer put a hand on my shoulder, his gaze also on the healing bullet hole. "Just a scratch, huh?"

I was trying to come up with some way to defend myself when Alex piped in, "It's from a hunting accident. Cool, right?"

"If by cool you mean idiotic," the irritated girl said from behind us. "What kind of idiot gets shot while hunting? What, you forget to wear orange or something?"

"Something like that," I replied in a dry tone. Traer turned away to hide a laugh and I slapped his shoulder. His laugh turned into a pained cough.

Ron, Dave, and two other members of the Search and Rescue team had a stretcher assembled and finished strapping Don onto it. Seth and Max waited in the shade of the canyon with their tongues lolling out and pleased expressions on their faces. One of Ron's girl teammates had brought them water and was making a big deal out of them. I refrained from telling her they had missed the trail entirely and vowed instead to give them extra chores when we got back to wipe the smugness from their faces.

"Hup," Ron called. His team lifted the stretcher and they started out ahead of us. Traer conversed with the team's medical lead while the wolves gamboled on ahead wagging their tails and looking like foolish dogs.

"You'd think they found a missing city the way they act," Nora said with a quiet laugh.

I glanced at her. "Too bad they lost the trail halfway in."

She gave me a puzzled look, then a small smile. "Traer said you were the best tracker."

I shrugged. "It's the reason I went on ahead. Sorry about ditching you back there."

"I didn't want to slow you down. I just can't believe you went down into that cave without ropes." She gave me an unreadable look that made me uncomfortable.

I lifted an eyebrow. "Would you believe I did it for the

thrill of the adventure?"

She shook her head. "I believe you did it to help innocent humans who were hurt." Her eyes narrowed. "I don't understand you, Vance."

"That I'm not all evil?" I asked offhandedly to cover up how much her words bothered me.

"That you live in a desert, have a Masters degree in Literature and Philosophy, and take care of a pack of werewolves instead of living a normal life in the city." Her brow creased. "There're a lot of werewolves that function in society."

I didn't let my surprise show. "Are you saying that you're okay with werewolves in normal society?"

She avoided my gaze. "I don't know what I believe anymore," she said softly.

I let that settle for a moment, then brought out the topic that had been at the back of my mind all day. "It's a full moon tonight."

The skin around her eyes tightened slightly at the thought of being surrounded by a group of werewolves forced to be in wolf form by the moon. She brushed at an imaginary speck on the sleeve of her shirt. "Does, uh, your pack generally behave on full moons?"

I nodded and fought back a smile at the tension in her voice. "They do, and we're not a pack."

She glanced at me. "What do you mean?"

I shrugged. "Two's more of a werewolf retreat than a pack territory. The wolves at Two are my friends, but five male Alphas living together along with nine other male grays isn't exactly natural." My heart turned over at the thought that with the help of Nora's Hunters, the numbers were actually four Alphas and six grays.

"Then why do you live there?"

I phrased my answer carefully. "Two was created to be

our second home, a haven where male werewolves could grow up in safety to preserve the werewolf line."

"Females are expendable?" Nora asked with a spark of defiance.

I chuckled. "Not exactly. The females are safe. Someone started killing off Alphas when I was six. My parents built Two as a sanctuary." My tone darkened. "Eventually, it became easier to just keep us here. Alphas are a bit hard to live with."

"Did they visit?" she asked, horrified.

"For a while." I forced a nonchalant tone. "Then we communicated through computer and phone."

"And they feel justified in abandoning their children to raise themselves?"

I studied the rock walls around us. "When someone else started killing off Alphas again a year ago, and were much more successful at it this time, it justified their system." My throat tightened, but I forced my voice to remain steady. "I was supposed to go home when I turned eighteen, but the first killings happened just before my birthday, and one of their gifts was that I would stay at Two until it was safe."

Nora glanced at me out of the corner of her eye. "And who decides that?"

I didn't answer and she didn't press the issue.

After a while, she said, "There must be something more that keeps you at Two besides your parents."

I nodded and gestured to the red rocks around us. "This keeps me."

She shot me a look. "Dirt and rocks?"

I shook my head and pointed at the achingly blue sky above the stark red sands. "The azure sky, the red sandstone, the cool nights and hot days. I'm free out here in my own way."

"And trapped as well," she replied. She held up a hand

when I opened my mouth to argue. "Don't get me wrong. You can have your blue sky and rocks and all, but this isn't freedom."

"And you have freedom?" I pressed.

She glared at me and turned away in a huff. We walked in silence back to the vehicles, then said goodbye to Ron and his team.

"Another find to make me look bad," Ron said good-naturedly as he shook my hand.

I grinned. "You just started missing me, that's all."

He rolled his eyes and opened the door to my jeep. The wolves jumped in and Nora started to climb gingerly up after them, but Traer stopped her and motioned toward the front seat. Nora glanced back at me in surprise. I shrugged to hide my own astonishment. She limped around the jeep and climbed into the front seat, then threw Traer a grateful smile.

He met my eyes with a slight touch of red to his cheeks and got in the back with Seth and Max. I bit back a smile and started the engine.

# Chapter 6

It felt good to phase in the light of the moon. I chose to do it outside away from Nora so as not to scare her. She was adamant that she wouldn't try to leave, and I hoped the idea of nine wolves running around was enough to keep her from taking back her promise.

Brian, Ben, and Thomas, the other three Alphas at Two, joined me for our usual run around the perimeter. The six grays, Max, Seth, Traer, Johnny, Zach, and Drake, followed close behind. It was a silent, formidable group, but my bones ached deep inside for a real pack and the closeness and loyalty that came from running with a true family. My own parents, Alphas themselves, had only run with me once for my first phase at Two when I was seven. The other werewolves around me had similar stories, and we had learned to rely on ourselves for friendship and camaraderie, a hard thing when most males branched out to start their own packs in their late teens and early twenties. It stung to be forbidden even my rights as an Alpha, though the gaping absence of the other wolves who should be with us was a stark remind of my failure to them as well.

I shook my head to clear the dark thoughts and broke into a run. I veered away from the others and loped across the soft desert sand through red rock walls that twisted and branched to the point where loss of attention to the path meant getting lost and possible death by starvation and thirst if not by rattlesnakes.

I loped through scrub brush and down winding game trails until I left the other werewolves far behind. I cut across the path of our jeeps from the day before and followed them at a breakneck speed. I didn't slow until I reached the mouth of White Horse Canyon. The scent of death touched my nose before I traveled half a dozen feet along the narrow trail. The jeeps would have had to take it easy here with their cargo. I pushed the thought aside and padded through the salt grass and rocks that lined the meager trail.

The canyon turned to the west to follow the river that had once been great enough to carve its deep channel, but now trickled along the bottom until swelled by the occasional flash flood to cover the trail. I followed it a short distance, then turned up a deer trail that smelled of Zach, Max, and lifeless bodies. They must have carried them one or two at a time up the winding trail to the canyon hidden behind.

I took a steeling breath, then topped the rise. My stomach turned and breath caught at the sight and smell of twenty-four bodies in the ravine below. I was responsible for fourteen of their deaths. I swallowed and forced myself to look at them. Faces of young men and women around the age of the werewolves at Two stared unseeing at the full moon. Several of the girls were beautiful. I could imagine suitors kissing their cheeks and working up the courage to ask for a dance. The men reminded me of soldiers sent off to war, barely old enough to hold a gun, yet entrusted with the lives of those on either end. I pictured mothers saying farewell and fathers telling their sons how proud they were.

A lump formed in my throat. Sorrow rose so strongly I couldn't hold it in. The agony I felt over Sam's death and the death of the other werewolves at Two battered against my mind and thoughts until I couldn't think any longer. The fact that other families would feel the same loss for the Hunters below made my bones ache. I lifted my nose to the moon and howled for the lives that would never be lived because of a foolish decision to attack a werewolf hideout.

A few minutes later, nine other voices rose to mingle with mine, their howls as dark and raw as my own with the loss of our companions. We said goodbye to them as wolves letting go of trusted comrades, saying farewell to boys we had grown up with and watched mature, of memories wasted and lives thrown away. We might not have made a proper pack, but when our parents took the easy way out of raising us, we stood by one another and helped each other through the hard times.

I let the guilt I felt at not being prepared for the attack tangle in my voice. I was the leader of Two. I accepted responsibility for their deaths and for the loss of the Hunters in the ravine beneath my feet. The heaviness on my shoulders threatened to choke me and my voice died away while the others continued to echo through the countless canyons. They, too, eventually faded, leaving the desert sands fuller and more empty with their passing.

I studied the bodies below until their faces blurred into one and Sam's empty eyes stared back at me. A drop of water fell on my head, shaking me from the memory. I blinked and rose, the rare desert rain falling like tiny stars laced with moonlight. The moon was starting its descent in the sky, casting a halo of silver from behind clouds that had gathered while I was lost in my thoughts. I closed my eyes and relished the moon's embrace for a moment, then forced myself to turn toward home.

It was hard to leave the bodies of the Hunters, strangers who had come with the intent to kill us, but who were nonetheless sons and daughters, brothers and sisters, and perhaps lovers whose bodies wouldn't be mourned or buried like they deserved.

I ran away from thoughts that would be treated as outrageous back at Two. I thought of Sam, Riff, Jason, and Sy, once full of life, hope, and dreams, and now just bodies that would be taken home in the morning for their own loved ones to mourn. I regretted that I couldn't go with them and wish their families the condolences and respect they deserved, but I didn't dare leave Nora to the whims of the others if a vengeful mood came upon them. A group of wolves could be worse than a mob if fueled by the right type of rage.

I arrived back at Two to find Nora gone, her scent hours old. A pit formed in my stomach, but I wasn't surprised. I picked up her trail amid the rain just outside camp where Brian had been stabbed in the leg. His blood colored the sandy ground in a dry dark patch that would soon be washed away by the rain. Fear didn't color Nora's scent, only anxiety and urgency so I knew no one was chasing her. She had chosen the perfect night for her escape, the only night when I didn't post sentries at Two because usually no one was there to worry about.

I loped along her trail, her scent growing stronger and stronger until I made out her form stumbling through the shadows. She glanced back, but her gaze moved past my black fur camouflaged in the darkness. She wiped rain from her forehead and continued around the corner. I trotted to catch up to her, then stopped.

She stood in the middle of the trail and glared at me with her hands on her hips. "I'm not going back," she said in a tone edged with the slightest hint of fear.

I wondered if she had ever seen a phased werewolf before. We looked like normal wolves, but bigger. A phased werewolf weighed the same as in human form because mass wasn't lost during the phase, just relocated, which made for some quite intimidating animals, and I was the biggest werewolf of any I had met.

I sat down on the trail and watched her, weighing my options. The rain fell around us with a patter that sounded like tiny feet, turning the dusty ground into plastered mud while the few plants soaked in what they could reach.

I couldn't phase back to human form until the moon sunk below the horizon, so I could either drag her back unwillingly in my wolf form, facing who knows what kind of battering she was capable of after the last several assaults I had experienced, or I could go with her, make sure she was safe, then convince her to return with me after the moon had lost its hold.

I rose and walked slowly through the rain to her side. She stiffened and I could tell she forced herself not to run. A twist of her fear tangled on the night breeze and a pang ran through me at the thought that she had seen so much of what we really were and was still afraid. I gave a soft snort and passed her on the trail. It surprised me how hard it was to turn my back on her with her Hunter background even after what I knew of her. I fought back a wry smile at our similarities, reminding myself that a wolf's smile looked a bit more menacing than a human's.

"Where are you going?" Nora demanded from behind me.

I kept walking, knowing she had no choice but to catch up.

Her feet thudded on the path and she huffed when she grew near. "What? You going to walk me to my dad's?" The heavy sarcasm held a hint of hope.

I was grateful I couldn't answer in wolf form and kept walking. She caught up to my side, then fell in step at the far side of the path. We walked for several minutes in silence. The breeze brought me her subtle scent of vanilla and sunflowers touched with rain. She studied the moon, the stars, the landscape around us, everything to avoid looking directly at me. I almost gave up and walked away when she cleared her throat softly.

"It's nice not walking alone," she said in an uncertain voice. The rain pattered around us lightly, but the darkness of the clouds to the east indicated heavier rainfall at higher elevations. I wondered how she dared to walk through a night where even the full moon was obscured by clouds and the rain sounded like a hundred creatures waiting just out of sight.

I glanced at her. She stared straight ahead, but her hand strayed over and rested on my back. I walked on as though I didn't notice, but a surge of warmth ran from the spot on my back and down my legs, making them weak. I wondered at the strength she had over me and what she represented. My mother had pretty much threatened to come over and kill her for me, and I had no doubts what Nora's parents would do if they ever found Two.

I kept seeing her eyes that first night in camp, wide with pain but fierce with determination. When she looked at me, I smelled fear, but also an edge of defiance and courage that I admired. Her look had pierced right through me and wrapped around my heart. I shouldn't have saved her from the others, but at that point, it was the only course of action available to me. The heat from her hand and the tremor that ran through my skin at her touch scared me. I needed to keep my wits about me and I couldn't let her make me so vulnerable. Yet here we were, walking through the night against all logic, and I still felt weak under her touch.

If she felt anything strange she didn't show it, but she kept her hand on my fur. I didn't know if it was for comfort or because my eyesight was better in the dark. I was glad that as a wolf I couldn't ask. The emotions that warred inside me were conflicted enough without adding her hostility. We continued on through the desert rain, two strangers with more in common than either dared to admit.

\*\*\*

The moon set and the gray edge of dawn showed on the eastern horizon. The rain continued to fall softly, but the dark clouds in the distance told of rains that hadn't let up. Nora's hand eventually lifted and I knew she realized I was no longer forced to stay a wolf.

The closest clothing cache among those hidden along the landscape for emergencies wasn't too far away. I figured I could run to it, phase, dress, and reach her again before she got too far. I padded to the edge of the trail, glanced back to find her watching with an expression of loss and determination that sent a pang of regret through my heart, and disappeared into the sage.

I ran to the clothes hidden in a waterproof pack between two small boulders over the next ridge, phased, pulled on a pair of shorts, and ran back to the trail. She was gone as I had expected. Her footprints left the trail and headed sharply downhill to disappear over a stone rise. I climbed it and hurried down to find her at the edge of a natural chasm.

She glanced back and her eyes widened before she started to work her way to the bottom.

"I wouldn't do that," I warned.

She glared up at me, her green eyes sparking. "Go home, or run away from a beast?"

Her words cut like knives and I fought back the urge to bare my teeth and snarl. "It's raining. These gorges carry flash floods through the desert. If you're caught at the bottom, you might never get out."

"Oh, I'm so scared," she said. She rolled her eyes and slid to the bottom. As if to prove her point, she walked down the ravine.

The sound of water touched my ears and my heart slowed. "Get out of there."

59

She stopped. "If you come down here, I'll cut you again," she warned. She brandished a knife and I bristled at an answering echo of remembered pain that ran down my back.

I gestured up the hill. "If the water reaches you, I won't be fast enough to get you out."

An emotion flickered in her eyes too fast for me to catch, then she smiled. "You're just trying to scare me." She turned to continue walking, but stopped when the rush of water reached her ears. She turned back and the world slowed. "Vance?" she asked.

A raging river of water rushed around the corner above her carrying logs and debris torn from the ground by its heedless descent. Her eyes widened and she screamed. The plunging wall of water swallowed her before I could move.

"Nora!" I yelled.

I ran along the bank, fighting to keep her in view despite the debris that battered her body and the sage and twisted bushes that impeded my flight. I pushed myself to run faster than I ever had before. I rounded the next bend and my heart slowed at the roar of water that plummeted toward the edge of the ravine that led to a deep wash below. I glanced back in time to see Nora forced under the water by branches entangled around her. There was only one way to save her.

I slid down the side of the chasm. Gnarled roots and branches grabbed at my hands and body, then I pushed off and landed at the edge of the ravine. A puff of dust rose at my feet as though mocking the water that plummeted toward me. Sound dropped off the edge of the cliff at my back, a fall that would kill us both if I made any mistakes. The water roared closer, its sound multiplied by the chasm walls and the debris that was propelled by the water's maddening rush. I braced myself across the opening and gritted my teeth.

The first rush of muddy water surged past, then the branches, small tree trunks, and other debris that had been torn free by the raging water slammed into my body with a force that tore the air from my lungs. I held on and felt for Nora's body. An arm caught around my neck, then she was cradled against my chest, her small weight nothing compared to the force I held back. I pushed slowly to the side, inching slowly backward with the weight of the debris that pounded against us. I turned my back on it to protect Nora and felt the bite of broken branches against my bare skin.

One exceedingly sharp pain tore into my side. I ground my teeth to keep from crying out and reached the edge. The earth gave way when I grabbed onto it with my free hand and we dunked back under the water. I pushed against the bottom of the ravine with my feet and we surged back to the surface. I used the momentum to lever Nora onto the bank above.

I clung to several gnarled roots that had worked their way through the dirt, but I didn't have the energy to pull myself over. The water grabbed at my waist, trying to drag me along with it. I pressed my face against the dirt, relishing in my exhausted delirium the scent of forest loam, the cinnamon-laced touch of the desert sand, and the roughness of the roots under my hands.

Another log hit my body. My grip loosened and I almost let go, then hands wrapped around my wrist and pulled. Nora's strength wasn't enough, but her touch sent a surge of adrenaline through my muscles. I pulled with her, working my bare feet into the scratchy dirt and pushing against the branches and debris that tried to drive me back under. I heaved up with a grunt and used my remaining energy to pull myself higher. I rolled onto the bank with a sigh of relief.

"Do you have a death wish?" she demanded, her face above mine and her chest heaving.

"Do you?" I asked, fighting to catch my breath.

She let out a relieved laugh and collapsed on the ground next to me. "Maybe I do," she admitted. Sorrow touched her tone. "Maybe watching all of your friends die will do that to you."

I nodded, staring up at the trees above us. "Maybe so." I couldn't quite catch my breath. A nagging feeling gnawed at the back of my mind, but I pushed it away and turned my head to face her. "Are you okay?"

She checked herself over, then nodded. "Definitely bruised, but yeah, I think I'm alright. You?"

"I'm fine."

She pushed gingerly to her feet, then held out her hand. I took it and rose, but a shard of pain laced through my side so sharply it brought me back to my knees.

"Vance?"

I ran a hand along my bare back and felt something protruding from my right side.

"Vance, what's wrong?" Nora asked with fear in her voice. She leaned around me to see, then her hand flew to her mouth.

I put a hand on the ground to keep from falling over. My vision swam and dark spots danced at the edges. I fought to catch my breath, but the branch that had been driven deep by the raging water inhibited each intake of air. I grabbed the wood tightly and pulled.

"I don't think you should do that," Nora said. Her tiny hand covered mine.

"I can't heal if something's obstructing the wound," I forced out, breathing through clenched teeth.

"But you could bleed to death before you heal," she protested.

My vision narrowed to a dim tunnel. I pulled on the branch. For a moment, it wouldn't move, then it slid slowly from the wound with a sound like a boot pulling clear of mud. Blood flowed down my side. I collapsed on the ground.

Nora rolled me over. Her face floated inches above mine,

her green eyes bright with concern. "You can't give up," she said, her voice strangely muffled in my ears. "Your werewolves won't be able to find us out here."

Her logic warred with the overwhelming urge to close my eyes. She must have seen it on my face because her jaw set and determination burned in her gaze. She grabbed my arm and tried to pull me up, a tiny force considering my size, but the look on her face brought me slowly to my feet.

I held my side and felt the blood streaming out thick and hot through the gaping hole. My legs barely held me and I felt weaker than I ever had before. "I can't," I said, ashamed at the pathetic strength of my voice.

"You can and you will," Nora replied stubbornly.

She took a step and I stumbled beside her, then righted myself with a great effort. I gritted my teeth against the pain in my side and closed me eyes. I felt her take another step and willed myself forward beside her.

I don't know how many paces I took before my strength left completely. I fell against one of the contorted, knobby trees that made up the landscape, but before I could land on the ground, Nora was there. She eased me gently to my knees, her fingers soft and spreading heat wherever she touched me.

"You've got to hang in there," she said; her chiding tone didn't cover up the concern in her eyes as I lay back in the dirt and felt it cling to the wound.

I took a shallow breath and winced at the resounding pain. "Now's your chance to escape," I said in a strangled voice that barely sounded like me.

Her eyes held mine. She mouthed my name over and over, but I couldn't hear her. I closed my eyes. Her fingers slipped into my hand and I tried to hang on, but the darkness swept me away like the torrential river we had survived.

# Chapter 7

A sharp throb through my side awoke me. The familiar scent of the small medical room at Two touched my nose with the tang of antiseptic, cotton bandages, Traer's coffee, and the always-present cinnamon earth tones of the red rock walls. I kept my eyes closed. The memory of the river debris barreling down at me replayed again and again in my memory. Nora's hand showed through the rubble and I reached for it.

I opened my eyes and found Traer smiling down at me. "You finally decided to wake up?"

I lifted a hand to rub my eyes; it took more effort than I was used to. "How long was I out?"

"Two days," he replied, the tightness of his eyes revealing how worried he had been. Footsteps came down the hall. He glanced up, then looked back at me with a strange expression on his face. "Pretend you're still asleep."

"Why?" I asked, confused.

"Just do it," he said quietly before turning.

"How is he?" Nora's voice felt like a balm to my soul. She had stayed. She could easily have left me there and returned to her father. The rain would have erased her tracks and scent and she wouldn't have had to worry about pursuit. Instead, for some reason, she was still here.

"A little better," Traer replied with a kindness that surprised me.

A soft hand touched my cheek. I almost jerked back in surprise, but caught myself and held still. "His color looks better," she said softly.

"It does," Traer agreed.

"Do you think he'll wake up soon?" My heart slowed at the worry in her voice.

"I hope so," Traer replied. "I've done all I can. It's up to him now." He turned away and I heard the clink of metal instruments as he straightened them on the counter.

Nora's breath whispered close to my cheek, then her soft lips brushed my skin. "Come back to me," she said in a voice full of such quiet heartbreak I almost turned my head to kiss her back. She straightened and her footsteps faded from the room.

"It's touching the way she cares about you," Traer said quietly. I opened my eyes to see him watching me with a carefully emotionless expression.

"You tolerate her now?" I asked guardedly.

He nodded. "When the moon set and we phased back, we found that you both had left Two and figured that Nora had run and you went to bring her back. Brian, Ben, and I went after you, but the rain made tracking difficult. We almost gave up, then Ben saw Nora struggling through a pass."

His voice took on a peculiar tone. "She pulled you as far as she could and was on the verge of collapse. When we reached her, she told us what had happened and that she feared you were dying, which you were."

I nodded. I remembered the feeling of complete blackness, no warmth, no cold, only empty sadness at leaving something I couldn't remember. It was a sensation I never wanted to feel again.

"We patched you up and carried you back. Nora was so exhausted Brian carried her most of the way."

"Brian?" I didn't hide my shock. He was always the most volatile against Hunters, and he didn't bother to conceal his disapproval of Nora every time our paths crossed.

Traer smiled. "She tried to refuse his help. I think that's what won him over."

I laughed, then grabbed my side as pain knifed through it where the branch had been. Something twisted deep inside and nausea rolled through my stomach. Bright spots danced at the edges of my vision.

Traer's eyes darkened with concern and he unwrapped the bandages. I twisted gingerly to see the wound. The skin where it had been was pink with healing and would leave only a round scar the size of a golf ball where the stick had protruded, but he didn't look satisfied. "You were pretty messed up. All I could do was put things as close to right as I could and let your body do the rest." He hesitated like he didn't want to tell me something, then sighed and gave in. "I spoke to your mom about it." He rushed forward to fend off my frustration. "Your mother said there are cases where such wounds heal, but not as they should. Only time will tell if you've truly recovered."

I pushed myself up slowly, ignoring the throb in my side. "Then I guess we'll leave it to chance." I forced a smile, but Traer didn't return it.

He put a hand on my bruised chest. "You should probably take it easy. Being unconscious for two days doesn't exactly scream optimum health." He glanced down at the bruises. "Those should have healed by now. Rest is your best bet."

I gave a true smile at his concern. "Have you ever been able to convince me to listen to reason?"

He rolled his eyes and shook his head. "No."

I stood up from the table, then stumbled when my knees threatened to give out. I caught myself on the edge of the counter and threw him a look I hoped was confident. "I'm famished. What's for dinner?"

He sighed and led the way out of the room. I followed faster than my body wanted to keep up. I would pay for it later, but the wolf side of me refused to show weakness. I didn't know whether it was survival or stupidity that kept me walking when I wanted more than anything to go to my rooms and sleep, but I forced my feet to keep moving and followed Traer to the kitchen.

A surge of energy ran through my body at the sight of Nora and Seth chopping vegetables on the counter. Thomas, Brian, Drake, and Johnny sat on various surfaces around the kitchen talking and joking around. I leaned against the doorway and watched Nora reach over and adjust Seth's grip on the knife.

"Remember that you're slicing a cucumber, not someone's neck. Hold it softly, like this."

The other werewolves laughed and Seth turned bright red, but he gave her a grateful smile and proceeded to slice more gently. Johnny glanced over and saw us watching. His eyes widened and he jumped off the counter and cleared his throat. The others noticed and rose, too. Brian nodded at me, a slightly embarrassed smile on his face.

Nora said something to Seth, noticed he wasn't paying attention, then followed his gaze to me. Her eyes widened and the green of them sparkled in the kitchen light before they filled up with tears. "Oh, Vance," she said. She rushed over and threw her arms around my neck, hugging me so tightly I had to force my fight or flight instinct down so I didn't hurt her. She then stepped back and looked at me, a slight blush to her cheeks as though she realized she had crossed some unspoken line between us. "How do you feel?" she asked, still with an edge of excitement.

"I've been better," I replied honestly.

Traer lifted an eyebrow, but I ignored him.

A hush had fallen over the kitchen. Nora seemed unaware of it. "I'm so glad you're awake."

I glanced at the others and they all turned away and pretended to be occupied with other activities. Brian picked up the knife Nora left and chopped with surprising enthusiasm. Seth proceeded more carefully, though not with the same grace he had used under Nora's supervision. Johnny and Drake appeared suddenly interested in something in a bowl by the sink.

I gritted my teeth against a smile at their obvious diversions, but the look on Nora's face sent my heart plummeting. "What?"

"You stood on the edge of a cliff to save me from a flash flood. Who does that?"

I shrugged. "Werewolves?" I said as more of a question than an answer.

Brian shook his head from across the room. "I wouldn't."

We both looked at him and he sputtered, "I mean, I would for you now, but not for some stranger." At my look, his eyes widened. "I'm afraid of heights."

"I am a stranger," Nora pointed out, her eyes on mine.

"Not really," I replied. My heart did a strange flip at the way her gaze lightened.

"Well, I did shoot you," she replied, a teasing tone to her voice.

I nodded. "There's that."

Traer gave me an accusing look but didn't interrupt. Seth gave an audible gasp, then pretended like he cut himself with his knife. I couldn't take the searching look in Nora's eyes and changed the subject. "So what are you doing here?"

She looked like she wanted to argue and I realized she took the words wrong. I indicated the kitchen and another faint blush stole across her cheeks. She smiled with embarrassment. "Seth brought me some food yesterday and I could barely choke it down. I promised to teach them how to make a few more edible dishes."

Seth spoke quickly, "She made shrimp cabbage wraps and lemon meringue pie for lunch. It was excellent."

The others nodded and my nose identified the slight hint of lemon peel and cocktail sauce lingering on the dishes in the sink. "And now?"

"We're working on chicken cordon bleu with a side salad," Johnny said proudly.

I lifted my eyebrows at Nora and she shrugged. "I don't know how you have all survived this long."

"Lots of t.v. dinners," Brian put in helpfully.

I crossed to a stool on the other side of the counter and eased myself onto it gingerly. It hurt to sit up straight, but I didn't let it show. The others watched me until the silence became awkward. "Well, let's see if you can teach these animals how to cook," I prompted.

"With pleasure." Nora threw me a smile at the challenge and went back to the others.

Traer took a seat next to me and watched the cooking proceed. It felt strange to have a girl at Two. One of the rules my mother strictly enforced was that no girls were allowed on the premises. It felt like a boys only clubhouse, and many of the werewolves had girlfriends in the surrounding cities that they visited on occasion. Nora's presence softened the edges of Two, bringing warmth to the red rock walls and laughter to the hollow corridors.

I watched her fingers deftly knead the chicken in a batter of breadcrumbs and butter and wondered when the last time was that I watched a woman cook. Her hands paused and I looked up straight into her eyes. Her brows creased slightly, causing a tiny furrow to form between them. A touch of red stole across her cheeks, making her green irises stand out even more. I looked away and couldn't explain how just meeting her gaze made my heart race. Traer caught my look and lifted an eyebrow. I rose and pretended like my side didn't throb like a pit of burning fire.

"Where are you going?" Traer asked.

"Can't put off the inevitable much longer," I answered.

"Calling your mother?" he guessed with a sympathetic grimace.

Similar expressions crossed the other werewolves' faces when I nodded.

"Good luck," Brian said after me. "We'll be here not getting our ear chewed off."

I fought down a growl and left the room.

***

"So not only did you *not* kill her, you risked your life to save her and almost died because of it?" Mom's voice was two octaves higher than normal. I set the phone on the opposite side of the couch from me, but distance did nothing to improve the high pitch. "I should kill her myself and save you the trouble," she threatened. "What on earth are you thinking?"

"That I'm tired of people running to my mother and tattling," I said dryly.

"That you're keeping her around because she's pretty?" Mom shot back. "Ben told me, so don't you dare deny it." Her tone begged me to try.

"She's beautiful," I agreed, even though in my mind the word didn't come close to describing her eyes, or the way her face softened when she helped the others, or the soft blush that stole across her cheeks whenever I caught her watching me, which unsettled me as often as her.

"So you admit that you're keeping her for her looks," Mom said with a triumphant note.

"I admit that she's beautiful," I replied. "But her beauty has nothing to do with why she's here."

"Then why is she there?" Mom demanded. Her tone indicated I had pushed her to the last edge of her patience, a line I was finding easier to reach lately.

"I'll let you know when I figure it out," I replied, exasperated. I ran a finger over the calluses on my right hand and leaned my head against the back of the couch. "In the meantime, thanks for your concern about my health. Your motherly interest is touching."

"It would be more worthwhile if I had a son who acted according to his lineage," she snapped back.

We both fell silent and I could almost feel her regret

71

through the phone. I couldn't decide if it was remorse over her words or for a son who brought her so much disappointment. When several minutes passed without her saying anything, I finally hung up.

# Chapter 8

I was still resting on the couch when Nora's familiar footsteps sounded down the hall. She paused outside the door and I could hear her shifting her weight from foot to foot. A light sound touched the door, then she took a deep breath and turned the handle. I sat up and winced at the sharp pain that came from the movement, but I schooled my face not to show it when she stepped inside.

"You're awake," she said. The emotions in her eyes conflicted as though she wasn't sure if that was a good thing or bad.

I shrugged, then regretted it and leaned back. "Just recovering."

"From the stick?" she asked. She quickly crossed the floor to me as though worried I was going to pass out at any moment.

The thought made me chuckle shallowly. "From talking to my mother."

She grinned. "And I thought I was the only one with an exhausting parent." She sat down on the floor so that her back leaned against the couch by my legs. I resisted the urge to touch the shiny strands of long back hair that rested on top of the brown leather.

"Let me see," I said to distract myself. "I suffer from a case of mild parental neglect with sudden bursts of extreme controlling and long-distance concern. You?"

She shook her head and I could see the corner of her smile when she replied, "Nope. My dad's the opposite. He's overbearing, extremely protective, and determined that I'm going to get myself caught in a situation I can't get out of without him."

We both sobered at the thought that he might be right. I took a testing breath and let it out slowly. "My dad pretends that he doesn't have a son." My heart clenched at the words I hadn't admitted to anyone. I don't know why I told them to her, but the truth sounded so much harsher when spoken out loud. "When I moved here, he found it more convenient to forget about me than to keep up the exhausting job of staying in touch."

I waited for Nora to laugh or brush it off, but she didn't do either. Her fingers strayed to the hem of my pants near my bare feet and she toyed with the fraying cloth. The light brush of her hand against my skin made me close my eyes. Besides Traer patching me up occasionally, no one touched me, not even by accident. No one messed with the hulking werewolf who could break them in two. I wasn't sure I would know what to do with affection if I got it.

Unaware of my thoughts, Nora concentrated on her fingers. "My mother disappeared when I was young," she said in a voice as guarded and searching as I imagined mine had been. "My dad says she was killed by werewolves, which is why he became a Hunter. He never had proof of it, but he's spent his whole life protecting me and preparing me."

"For what?" I asked quietly.

"For them to try to take me, too." She let out a slow breath as though they were words she hadn't spoken out loud before either. "But it doesn't make sense to me. He's told me the story of her disappearance several times, but it doesn't add up and it changes every time he tells it."

"Have you tried pointing that out?" I asked cautiously. I worried she would stop talking and hide behind her defensive persona if I asked the wrong question.

She shook her head, then turned so I could see her face. Her fingers stayed knotted in the cloth of my pants as though it kept her grounded. "Can you imagine what it's like living with a father who's convinced his daughter is going to be killed by werewolves any day? I was escorted to school, then afterwards when other kids were at play dates or sleepovers, I learned how to clean a gun and make my own bullets. I owned my first twenty-two when I was eight, and could shoot it with a nickel's accuracy a year later." Her eyes studied the couch, her gaze hard as she saw past the leather. "I took martial arts, fencing, boxing, anything my dad thought would help me later. He didn't let me have any friends, and fired someone if they talked to me too long." She paused, the outrage she felt etched on her face.

"That's horrible," I said softly. My own problems with my parents diminished and I felt bad for snapping at my mother when she was only concerned for my wellbeing.

"That's why I went out with Jerome and the others. I wanted to get away and prove to my dad that I could handle myself." She gave a humorless laugh. "But look at me now."

I hesitated, but the loss in her eyes gripped my thoughts. I reached out a hand and put my fingers under her chin, tipping it up so she would look at me. "Nora, you saved my life. You could have given up on me and left, but you didn't. That's a daughter any father should be proud of."

Her eyes held her want to believe my words. I felt an echoing response in my heart for my own father's approval, to be able to go home again or live my life the way I wanted. Her lips eventually twitched up in a small smile. "I don't know if he would agree with me saving a werewolf."

"The werewolf you saved is grateful regardless," I responded.

She smiled her soft smile and turned her back to the couch again with a satisfied breath. Her hair brushed against my knee, leaving several strands hanging on the fabric of my jeans. This time, I steeled my nerves and reached out. Her black strands were as soft as her true smile. I let them play between my fingers and watched her shoulders tense when she realized what I was doing.

She turned slowly, her eyes on her hair in my palm. "Untying a knot," I lied.

She smiled and pushed up on the couch so that she sat next to me. She lifted a hand, then hesitated. My heart started to pound and I looked away, unsure I could trust the feelings that thundered through my mind. Her fingers touched my hair, soft at first, then with more confidence. I looked back and found her watching me, waiting to see my response. When I didn't say anything, her lips quirked at the corners. "I thought there might be a lion hidden under this golden mane."

I laughed in surprise, then winced before I could hide it. "Haven't seen a barber in a while," I admitted quickly to chase away the concern that flitted across her face.

Her fingers toyed with the dark blond strands that fell unruly across my forehead. "It suits you," she decided.

"Thank you," I replied. "I thought I was more of the bear type."

She shook her head, her eyes serious with only a hint of teasing laugh lines around the edges. "Only a lion could keep this pack under control. You've done a good job here."

A tremor ran up my spine at the words I had always longed to hear. Two was not an easy life, and the deaths of my comrades weighed heavily on my shoulders. Appreciation was far short with the tempers and compulsions of too many Alphas and headstrong grays living together. "It's nice to hear once in a while," I admitted.

She touched my arm, then lifted it up so she could lean against my uninjured side. I lowered my hand back down slowly and let it rest gently at her waist, hoping my fingers didn't tremble the way my heart did. "It's nice to be appreciated," she agreed, her head on my shoulder. I turned my face into her hair and closed my eyes as her heady scent of vanilla and sunflowers filled my nose.

I knew I was falling for her, and even the thought that she was a Hunter's daughter couldn't stop the way my heart pounded at her nearness. Werewolves mated for life. I wondered what Mom would say if she knew my heart was being stolen by the girl she loathed. I then realized with a start that she already guessed, and her vehemence against Nora was her way of protecting me.

I frowned into Nora's hair. She tucked her feet up underneath her and her breathing slowed into a light, steady rhythm. I needed to distance myself from her, but I couldn't leave the couch. Her presence was too comforting. I closed my eyes and let my head rest back, her quiet breathing a gentle counterbalance to the whirlwind of my thoughts.

\*\*\*

It took two days until I felt ready to spar again, and then I was pushing it. Drake and Zach ran through the forms with me. My body knew them without thought, but the pain in my side made it difficult to perform several of the moves. I ran through them carefully until I could push past the pain. The gray coats didn't comment at my slow progress and waited patiently for me to keep up.

After several hours had passed, Zach cleared his throat and I looked up to see Brian and Ben watching us from the door. "Up for a run, old man?" Ben asked.

"Anytime," I shot back. "And I'm only a year older than you."

Ben rolled his eyes. "We'll see about that." The brothers left and I heard Brian chuckle down the hall.

I punched the bag next to me. It hit the wall with a resounding thud, but the motion sent a slice of pain through my side so sharp my breath caught.

"You sure you should be phasing?" Drake asked. He kept his eyes on the velcro of his sparring gloves that he detached and fastened again.

It was all I could do to keep from attacking him. I had to remind myself that my frustrations were toward Brian and Ben, and most of all my injury that should no longer be bothering me. I let out a breath slowly and walked from the room without replying.

Traer caught up to me in the hall. "Phasing, really? Without need?"

"You know how it is," I cut him off before he could protest further. "I appreciate Drake and Zach running to my second mother for help."

Traer rolled his eyes. "They're concerned, as they should be. You need to take care of yourself."

"What I need is to not be undermined every time I turn around," I snapped back. A hurt look swept across his face and I regretted my harsh tone. I put a hand on his shoulder. "It might be foolish, but Two is mine and I have to uphold my authority or this place will be overrun. I'm not a weak pup who can sit by while others think they own everyone here." I softened my words with a smile. "It's just a run. Don't worry so much."

"Maybe you should worry more," Traer replied, but the anger had gone out of his words.

# Chapter 9

I pulled off my shirt and tossed it on a branch of the gnarled tree I crouched behind. My side already throbbed and my stomach twisted at the thought of phasing, but I was committed. Backing out now would definitely show weakness. I kept telling myself it was only a run and let my body phase slowly into wolf form.

Pain like a dozen hot irons scalded my side as my skin and organs took on the wolf shape. I breathed through gritted teeth and kept silent, but by the time the phase was complete, the pain was so intense I threw up on the red sand and had to lie on my side for several minutes until my strength returned.

A howl sounded and I forced myself to my feet. My limbs trembled, but I shook my coat against the pain and trotted out from behind the bushes. Ben and Brian waited on a rise, both heads turned in my direction. I hoped they hadn't heard me lose my lunch, but there was nothing I could do about it. I pushed the pain down and loped to join them. They turned without a sound and fell in on either side of me. It was then that I knew this wasn't going to be just an ordinary run.

I decided to draw them away from Two, knowing that if the others joined in, I would have no chance. I loomed above them, a bear-sized black wolf with a smaller black wolf running on each side. The weakness through my limbs threatened to steal my strength and running took every ounce of willpower to push past the driving pain. I ran around brush I would normally jump, and took the path up a sandy wash to save my energy. Sunlight bounced off the deep red sand, casting shadows at the base of scrub brush and sage. The azure sky looked like a bowl turned upside down, watching the scene unfold below with the impassivity of the everlasting.

The threat and hostility underlying the scent of the two wolves burned into my mind. They had fought for Two on several other occasions, but accepted defeat almost before we had begun. This time was different; their confidence and the looks they threw each other set my teeth on edge. It disgusted me that they waited until I was at my weakest to challenge me for Two, but I was determined to defeat them no matter what the cost.

The brothers waited until we were several canyons away from Two to attack. They darted forward as one, but I was ready when Brian dove at my front paws. I jumped over his head and spun so that I landed facing them both. Ben snarled and tried to bowl me over with a shoulder against my chest, but I was stronger than either of them even injured.

I grabbed the back of Ben's neck and threw him to the side. He landed against a rock and whined, then charged back with another snarl. Brian leaped at my back when I turned to meet Ben's attack. I rolled and broke his grip on my fur. He hit the ground, leaving a jagged tear across my shoulder.

Ben dove at my throat as I rose back to my feet, but I ducked my head and his fangs lacerated my forehead instead. I gave an inward sigh of thanks for the hard skull my mom always complained about and forced him back. I wiped the blood from my eyes with a paw to clear my vision and felt Brian's jaws close around my back leg. I spun and grabbed his throat before he could leap clear.

I forced him onto his back on the ground. He struggled for a moment and the scent of desperation wafted heavily in the air. I tightened my hold and Brian gave in. His tail curled up to his stomach and he held still. A whine escaped his throat.

Ben advanced from my other side, but the growl that rumbled through my chest stopped him. He may have wanted to attack me, but his brother's life hung by the pressure of my fangs. Instinct bade me to tear into him, to put all the rage and frustration of the past weeks into ripping out his throat; but I knew my responsibilities and the consequences of such an action.

I clamped down briefly to remind him who was in charge, then slowly let go and stepped back to allow him to rise. He cast a furtive glance in my direction and ducked behind Ben. Red showed on Ben's muzzle from my bleeding forehead. He met my eyes for the briefest second, then turned away. I watched until the two brothers left around the next bend. As soon as they were out of sight, my legs gave out and I collapsed on the ground.

The pain that knifed through my side had doubled, and maneuvering through the fight had intensified it until I could barely think. Blood leaked in my eyes. I wiped my face on my shoulder and debated whether to phase or try to make it back to Two as a wolf. I didn't know if I could even survive another phase. I clenched my jaw and limped slowly back the way we had come.

My fear was that Ben and Brian would attack again while I was weak, but either my bravado fooled them or they realized the stupidity of their actions because I didn't see them. The trek back to our camp felt twice as long. The sun pounded on my black fur with relentless fury, and the azure sky faded to a heartbreaking pale blue. The scent of sun-baked sage tickled my nose and I sneezed. Pure agony ripped through my stomach. I sat for five minutes convincing my legs to carry me despite the pain.

The outside doors at Two were designed to be pushed open by a nose or shoulder. I went to the little-used back door closest to my room and shoved it open, dismayed at how much strength it took. I limped down the hall to my rooms and was grateful to find that Nora had remembered not to shut the door all the way. I pushed it closed with my shoulder and made it to the middle of the living room floor before I collapsed. My body shuddered. I tried to keep from phasing, but lost control through the pain. The phase stretched my wounds and sent a dagger of pain through my side so sharp a yell tore from my lips. I curled in around my side and tried to remain conscious.

"Vance?" Panic filled Nora's voice. Her footsteps ran into the room and fingers touched my shoulder so softly I barely felt them. "Vance, what happened?"

She ran to the door and I listened to her footsteps fade away. I sat up and had the presence of mind to pull a blanket from the couch down to cover my nakedness. Two sets of footsteps returned and the door was shoved open. "Vance, I tried to warn-" Traer's eyes widened and he paused, his eyes on the blood streaming down my forehead.

"Not as bad as it looks," I forced out. Pain throbbed with every breath.

Relief flooded Nora's eyes and she smiled despite a tear that trickled down her cheek.

"It looks pretty bad," Traer replied. A muscle twitched in his jaw. "What on earth happened?"

"Brian and Ben attacked me."

The words sent a surge of anger through my limbs and I pushed up despite the pain. Both of them moved to help me, but I gave them a sharp look and they waited. I sat on the edge of the couch and tried to clear the pain and anger from my thoughts so I could think clearly.

"What are you going to do?" Traer asked softly after a moment.

A dark numbness filled my chest, black and angry. Betrayal. That was how it felt to be attacked by two of the werewolves I had grown up with. The fact that they waited until I was at my weakest showed a cowardice I had never taught them. Fury burned through my body and I grabbed a lamp from the end table and threw it across the room. It shattered against the wall and fell to pieces on the ground. The tinkling of broken glass reminded me of the wind chimes that used to hang on our porch during my brief childhood.

I sat back with my eyes on the mess I had made. The pain was a dull throb within my anger. "Throw them out."

"It's about time," Traer replied with a candor that surprised me. I glanced at him and he shrugged. "They're getting a bit big for their britches. Time they started to fend for themselves."

Traer lifted a bandage and I shook my head. I brushed a hand across the wound on my forehead and found that it was already healing. "I'll be fine," I said. Bandages were the least of my worries at the moment. Disagreement colored his eyes, but he knew better than to argue. "You know they won't go lightly."

The young doctor nodded. "And Max and Drake'll probably go with them. I can't speak for Thomas. There's no telling what he'll do."

The last Alpha of our group was surprisingly mild for his football player stature. Next to me, he was the largest member of the group, but he tended to keep out of disputes. When he did decide it was time to leave, he would go quietly; of that I was sure.

Something was bothering the gray werewolf. Frustration showed clearly on his face edged with something else. "What's wrong?" I asked.

"I think you need to see a real doctor."

"You are a real doctor," I pointed out. "And I'm healing."

He gave me a tolerant look and nodded his head toward my throbbing side and the bruises that spidered away from the scar. "A specialist, then."

"In the internal workings of werewolf organs? The

specialist would probably be a Hunter," I replied dryly. I glanced at Nora and regretted the statement. "I didn't mean it that way."

She smiled sadly. "Unfortunately it's true, at least for my Dad's faction. He'd probably heal you, then kill you just for the sport of it."

"Sounds pleasant," Traer said, his voice tight at the thought.

I tried to find a more comfortable position on the couch, then winced when another sharp pain surged through my side. Nora set a hand on my arm and Traer stepped closer. I rolled my eyes, but felt touched by their concern. "I'm alright, really."

"I'll believe it when I see it," Traer replied, but he turned away at my look. "I'm going to see if Seth's got dinner started." He smiled at Nora. "Maybe it'll actually be edible thanks to your tutoring."

"Who would have thought werewolves would be such eager students?" she asked with a laugh.

"We get a little bored here," Traer replied. He nodded at me and left the room.

I leaned against the couch and thought vaguely that the blood from my shoulder was going to ruin the leather. Nora watched me for a moment, then settled next to me and stared at the wall. "Why did you agree to go running with them?" she asked after a couple of minutes had passed.

"It sounded like fun," I replied as more of a question than a statement. I could feel her disapproving stare and sighed. "It's an Alpha thing."

"So because I'm not a werewolf I couldn't possibly understand it?" the accusation in her voice covered the hurt she felt at being left out.

I tipped my head to look at her. "Alphas grow up knowing that someday they'll be in charge of the protection and wellbeing of their own pack. We normally test our strength against our fathers and other members of their pack, making sure that we're ready for when we set out on our own."

"But you don't have a pack here," Nora said with dawning understanding in her voice. "You're left to pit against your peers. What were your parents thinking?"

I shrugged, then clenched my teeth at the resulting pain. "Maybe we would grow out of it, or they could put it off until we had our own packs and they wouldn't have to deal with it."

"They're shrugging off their responsibility." Anger touched her voice.

I felt a sudden need to defend my mother. No matter what I had gone through, she still acted like my mom long after Dad quit the charade that had become our lives. "They see it as protecting us. We safe here, fed-"

"If you can call it that," she cut in.

I continued, "We have clothes, food, shelter, and access to the finest schools by the internet as well as the connections to attend any of them electronically. Our needs are taken care of."

"Except emotionally," she pointed out.

My voice dropped. "Emotional security comes when Hunters are killing off every Alpha they can get their hands on and you're safe because your parents have the foresight to hide you away." I took a calming breath and said quietly, "Even when their friends are being killed."

She closed her eyes for a second; when she looked at me again there was something unreadable in them. Her hand reached up and she set it gently on my jaw. "You are their emotional security," she said quietly. "You tolerate this for them."

"They care in their own way," I replied past a tremble

through my limbs that had nothing to do with pain. I closed my eyes and turned my face into her hand. "Like I care." Her scent filled my nose and my head clouded past any other thought.

Her other hand touched my dark blond hair hesitantly, then her fingers tangled in it, brushing my ear and sending a surge of heat through my body. "You care so much," she whispered.

I opened my eyes and tried to think past the fog in my mind that came from being so close to her, but my brain refused to process anything but the nearness of her lips and the way her eyes peered into mine with such intensity, but also with a touch of fear that showed she was afraid of what could happen. An echoing surge of emotion rushed through my chest and it was all I could do to keep from kissing her. "We have to be careful," I breathed out haltingly.

"You're never careful," she replied with a smile that melted onto my lips.

The taste of her kiss sent such a strong surge of need and want through me that I could barely breathe. I kissed her back and felt the need echoed through her touch. Her hand drifted from my jaw to my chest and felt so hot against my bare skin I imagined that it left a red outline. I didn't care if such a mark lasted a lifetime.

My cell phone rang and jolted us back to reality. Our lips separated and we stared at each other, amazed at what had happened, at the gulf that had been crossed. The fact that she was a Hunter mattered little to me anymore. I saw the same realization in her eyes and the bashful way she lowered them to her hand on my chest.

She pulled it back and I longed for her touch again. The phone gave another insistent ring. "You better take it," Nora said quietly.

I didn't want to. I had never wanted to ignore the phone

more. Nora picked it up and handed it to me, expectancy and a touch of humor in her gaze. I shook my head. She laughed and flipped it open. I sighed and was about to hit the speaker phone button by habit, but remembered Mom's previous opinions regarding Nora and lifted it to my ear.

"Hello?"

"I'm calling to apologize for our conversation the other day," Mom said in a voice that sounded resigned and apologetic at the same time.

I smiled because she sounded the same way about every other time she called, usually because we both ended up saying things we weren't proud of. "I'm sorry, too. I have a knack for pushing your buttons."

"You do," she agreed without admitting that she was at fault for the conversation as well.

I took a shallow breath against a surge of pain through my side. "I'm kicking Ben and Brian out of Two today."

"What? Why?" Mom demanded.

"They attacked me when we were out running. They're trying for leadership of Two."

I could almost hear Mom's teeth grinding through the phone and knew neither werewolf wanted to see the look she had on her face. "I'm going to call their mothers," she said.

I fought back a laugh. "They're not kids, Mom. They're eighteen. It's time for them to leave anyway."

"Yes, but after all we've done for them, given them a safe place away from killers. . . ."

She paused and I knew the topic turned her thoughts to Nora. I spoke before she could. "I'm taking care of it, so don't worry. I'll let you know how it goes."

I was about to hang up the phone when she said with more concern than I could remember hearing from her, "Are you okay? Did they hurt you?"

I hesitated, then brought the phone back up. "I'm alright.

Nothing a night's rest won't heal."

"Traer told me your side is still giving you problems," she said.

A grim smile touched my lips. "He worries too much."

"You don't worry enough," she replied.

I rolled my eyes at the same words Traer had said before the run. "Maybe so, but it's working out. Let their parents know they might be seeing more of their sons soon."

"Good riddance," Mom said the words I felt.

I hung up the phone and Nora leaned against my shoulder. "You're a good son."

I shook my head. "Not really, but we both gave up pretending long ago. I think we understand each other better this way."

She sat in silence for a few minutes, then sighed.

"What?" I asked even though my stomach twisted at the direction I guessed her thoughts had taken.

"I miss my dad," she said, confirming my guess. "He worries, too."

After my conversation with Mom I didn't feel that I could rightfully deny her unspoken request. I held out the phone and her eyes lit up. "Really?"

I nodded. "Just remember how many lives are in your hands."

She sobered a bit, but dialed the number with a smile of anticipation. The phone rang twice, then a deep voice answered.

"Hello?"

"Daddy?"

"Noralie? Is that you?" Sharp relief colored his voice. "Are you okay?"

"I'm fine, Dad, and I'm safe."

"When the others didn't come back, we assumed the worst. We've been searching night and day, but it's like you vanished off the face of the Earth. Is everyone alright?"

The sadness in her voice broke my heart. "They're all dead."

His voice tightened. "What happened? Where are you? I'm coming to get you."

Nora's eyes flicked to mine. "That's not possible." She rushed on before he could argue, "We happened upon a werewolf hideout and Jerome thought we could take them. Everyone was killed and they were going to kill me, too, but one of the werewolves saved my life. He's keeping me safe."

"You're being held captive?" The anger that laced his voice sent a surge of adrenaline through my body. I rubbed my knuckles together and tried to stay calm. "Do you know where you're at? I'll find you and have them all destroyed. You'll be safe."

"Dad. Dad!" It took a minute for him to calm down.

Tears glistened in Nora's eyes at the fear in his voice. The longing that shone in them was unmistakable, and I knew I couldn't keep her at Two any longer. "I'll take you to him," I whispered. A pain close to that in my side ran through my heart at the thought of letting her go.

Her eyes widened and the tears that had sparkled in them fell down her cheeks. "Really?"

"You want to go home. I won't make you stay."

I forced a smile at the way her eyes brightened and she told her dad, "Vance says he'll take me to you. I can come home!"

He fell silent for a minute and when he cleared his throat, I realized he had also been crying. I hated myself for the pain I had put them through, and felt equal pain for the families of all the Hunters that lay dead in White Horse Canyon. When her father spoke again, his voice was slightly unsteady. "Where can I meet you?"

She looked at me, her eyes searching mine. I thought

quickly. "Four Corners," I said. It was hours away and would throw him off if he tried to search for us. "We can meet him at sunrise."

"Sunrise at Four Corners," she repeated with such enthusiasm my heart ached. She met my gaze and her smile faltered. "But Dad, I want your word that Vance won't be hurt and he'll be allowed to go back home without anyone following him."

I frowned, but she waited for her father to reply. He took a breath. "He'll be protected; you have my word."

"Dad," Nora said with a sudden sternness that said she knew her father well. "He saved my life and I want to make sure he isn't hurt. If he'll be in danger, I won't come."

I pictured him making a face like my mom when I argued. He replied in a tight, controlled voice, "He'll be safe. I promise."

I didn't believe him, but Nora smiled. "Thank you, Daddy. I'll see you tomorrow morning."

"I'll be there," he vowed.

She hung up the phone, then threw her arms around me with such vigor my breath caught at the pain. "Thank you so much," she said. "I can't describe how much it means to me to see him again." She realized what she was doing and dropped her arms. The blush touched her cheeks again. "Sorry. I forgot."

I gave a weak smile. "It's alright." I studied the red rock wall across from us. "So. Tomorrow, huh?" I said after a minute.

She smiled. "Yes, tomorrow." She gave me a warm smile. "Thank you very much, Vance. I don't know how to repay you."

My eyebrows rose. "Maybe by not letting your dad kill me?"

She laughed. "It'll be okay, don't worry."

But I wasn't so sure.

"Come on tough guy," Nora said, rising from the couch. She held out a hand. "Let's get you cleaned up."

I grunted with the pain of standing. Nora slipped under my arm and helped me limp to the bathroom. I stood in the shower, then jerked back as water hit me. I had expected Nora to go, but she stood behind me with a white washrag in one hand. "Don't worry," she said with a teasing gleam in her eyes. "I'm just going to help you wash off the worst of it."

The blanket around my waist hung soaked and tattered, but I kept a tight hold on it. Somehow, being in the shower with Nora at my back made me feel more vulnerable than I had ever been in my entire life. She waited a minute, then the soft fibers of the rag worked slowly over the tear in my shoulder from Brian's teeth. The water that pooled around my feet turned red before rushing down the drain. My legs felt suddenly weak. I leaned my forehead against the cool tile of the shower wall and closed my eyes.

Nora stopped. "Are you alright?"

I nodded, but couldn't find the words to speak.

"Want to sit down?" Nora asked.

I backed up and she helped me slide down to sit so the water hit my chest. I hated that I was so vulnerable and weak in front of her that I needed her assistance to sit down. She could kill me with a single shot, regardless of how bad her aim had been the last time. Yet she tended to me. The thought curled around my heart and confused my thoughts. I ducked my head on my knees, careful to keep the blanket in place. Nora knelt beside me, and after a minute she continued washing my shoulder.

"Sorry," I said quietly. "I just got dizzy."

"You've lost a lot of blood," she replied. "Are you sure you don't want Traer to look at these?"

I nodded and sat back. She moved to wash my face

without care for how the water drenched her clothes and hair. Her sunflower and vanilla scent held the cinnamon and sage smell of the red rocks. It suited her, but I refrained from saying it.

I closed my eyes as she worked on the gash and fought back a smile when she muttered something about me not taking good enough care of myself. "As I recall," I said quietly. "I found you in here not too long ago."

I opened my eyes to find her watching me, a slight smile on her face. "That was different."

Her searching look made me feel bare, exposed in ways I couldn't hide. I studied the blood that pooled from the fang marks around my ankle. I forgot that it had been bitten. The blood trickled down my skin and touched the water with red before it swirled away and was washed out, forgotten. I felt much the same way before Nora came along. Now, her presence was too near and too real. I gave her everything without thought of how it would work out. Now she was leaving.

"I can take care of the rest," I said quietly without meeting her eyes.

"Are you sure?" she asked.

When I didn't answer, she rose and stepped out of the shower. She hesitated in the bathroom, then the door closed. A growl escaped my lips and I hit the floor of the shower hard enough to shatter a tile. I stared at the remains of yet another mess I had created. Water pooled around the dent and I imagined it seeping down into the sand below Two, giving life to something in need.

I rose and steadied myself with a hand against the shower wall when my knees threatened to buckle. I let the water run through my hair as I wondered what I had gotten myself into. Werewolves mated for life, but the girl who had stolen my heart was human. She wouldn't feel the same pain at leaving me. I tried to convince myself that she cared, but the fact remained that she would be gone come morning, and Two would be an empty shell without her presence to fill it.

# Chapter 10

Later that night, my lips curled back at the smell of Brian and Ben returning from their run. Adrenaline fueled by rage coursed through my body. I checked to make sure Nora was asleep, then stalked down the hallway to the main living area. I paused in the doorway to see Brian, Ben, Drake, and Max laughing together while Ben related a story to the others.

Ben's hand was raised mid-gesture when my scent finally registered. He froze and turned. I wondered how well he would do on his own, then realized I didn't care anymore. I had given them too much for them to turn around and attack me. It showed cowardice by both brothers, something I would never tolerate.

"Get out," I growled.

Brian and Drake turned while Max jumped up from his chair so fast it fell over. Brian looked like he wanted to protest, but Two was mine and I wasn't about to be contradicted. I spoke in a low growl, "Get out, or I'll tear you to shreds and send you home in a box. It's your choice."

"Is that any way to talk to a friend?" Ben asked, his face white but his eyes holding mine with an Alpha challenge.

"I would never talk to a friend like that," I said in a dangerous tone.

Brian bared his teeth in a humorless smile. "It's not our fault you weren't up for a run."

The fire that ran through my limbs chased away any pain. "You want to act like animals, I'll treat you like them." I phased so quickly they didn't have time to react. A loud rumble tore from my throat to echo through the red walled tunnels. I could hear other werewolves coming to see what was going on, but all I cared about was that Two was my sanctuary to protect, and the Lopez brothers had dirtied it long enough with their trouble and unrest. I was tired of being patient, of sheltering those who didn't care how good they had it, and of watching my back knowing that someday they would attack. I snarled and both Alphas backed up.

"Fine," Ben said, his tone light as he pretended he wasn't intimidated. "We'll go, but only because we're tired of Two and your pathetic attempts to act as everyone's parent to make up for your own."

I stalked toward them slowly, my teeth bared, hackles raised, and a low growl that sounded like thunder grating in my chest. Both Alphas and the two grays behind them left the room to gather their belongings. I waited at the exit to Two, my chest tight and the wounds from their teeth throbbing in a constant reminder of why I was chasing out boys I had grown up with.

Ben and Brian walked out with unconvincing nonchalance, while Drake and Max hurried after them throwing worried glances in my direction. It hurt a bit that the grays would go, but there were too many males at Two and the fewer egos, the better. The grays knew better than to butt heads with me directly, but their internal meddling and constant bickering with the other grays made their departure easier to accept.

Brian waved with a sardonic smile at the edge of camp, then the group disappeared through the red pillars into the starlit night.

I sat down and breathed easier for their absence. I worried about them because I felt responsible for their wellbeing, but it was good to let them go and not worry about being jumped in my own home. I waited until a jeep engine roared to life, then listened to it fade into the cacophony of desert insects, the howl of the wind through the myriad of caves along the top of the red rock ridges, and the cold chill that crept like a finger of icy flame to steal the warmth that remained of the day's sunlight.

I took a breath of the night air so familiar I knew it better than my mother's scent; sometimes my brain linked the two because it had been so long since I had actually seen her. I sighed and padded softly back through the tunnel to my quarters.

***

I shrugged gently and Nora lifted her head. "We're here," I whispered.

She blinked groggily, then perked up when she remembered what we were doing. She peered out into the parking lot and pointed at the lone truck waiting near the other end. "That's him!" she said.

I chuckled at her enthusiasm. "I assumed as much, seeing as it's the only other vehicle here."

She shoved my shoulder, but was too happy to say anything.

I pulled up a few rows away and put the jeep in park. Nora opened the door, then hesitated and turned back. My breathing slowed at the look on her face. "I'm not leaving for good," she said; she sounded like she wanted to convince us both. "I have your number and I'll call as soon as we get home." She glanced back toward the truck. "Even if Dad is against the idea."

I watched her, unsure of what to say. I had never been great at goodbyes because they were too final in my life. I gritted my teeth against a surge of regret.

She touched my face and her eyes held mine. "I'll be back," she promised. "Nothing could keep me away from you." My heart rose with her words and she kissed me, her lips parting mine. I breathed in her scent as we kissed, and felt surrounded by every part of her. Her fingers lingered on my shoulder where she could feel the scar of the bullet through my thin shirt. "I'll make up for that," she promised with a quiet breath.

She looked as if she wanted to stay, and for the briefest second I hoped that she would tell me to turn the jeep around and go back to Two. She looked at the other vehicle, torn, and we both knew she had to leave. "Go," I said quietly past the lump in my throat.

"I don't want to," she replied. The heartache in her voice held me fast.

"It'll be alright. I'll see you again soon."

She nodded at the words she needed to hear. She pushed open the door and ran across the pavement, her scent a sweet reminder as her kiss lingered on my lips. The door to the black truck opened and a tall man with thick muscles barely contained by his tailored suit climbed out. He held open his arms and she crumbled into them. I could hear what she said to him even through the distance and the windshield, but I ignored it to give them their privacy.

Foreboding rose in my chest. I studied the landscape around us, but nothing appeared out of the ordinary. I turned my attention back to Nora's father's truck. The sun rose slowly behind it, casting the plateaus around us in a wash of red and gold. I blinked into the rays, wondering if he had chosen the position strategically. My eyes focused and my heart slowed at movement from one of the back windows.

A barrel glinted in the light an instant before a bullet slammed through the jeep's windshield and into my arm. Nora screamed and I gazed at the hole in shock. My survival instincts kicked in above the dull pain. I opened the door and slid to the ground, then crawled to the back of the jeep amid the ricochet of more bullets that peppered the pavement around my hands and feet. Glass flew everywhere as the windows shattered above me. Shards fell to the ground and bounced around my hands, catching the light of the rising sun. Bullets tore through the metal doors with a sound like a tin can ripped open and amplified a hundred times by my sensitive hearing.

The rocks on the pavement bit into my hands and knees. The jeep tipped as the right front tire was shot, followed shortly by the left. Metal rang out when they hit the brush guard; bullets sunk into the engine with echoing thuds. My heart thundered in my chest.

I leaned against the jeep and tried to catch my breath. Pain surfaced from my arm and my side, but it was dulled by the surge of adrenaline through my veins. I forced myself not to phase, worried that Nora was in danger, too. I waited until the spray of bullets stopped, then peered around the edge of the jeep.

Nora's dad had a firm hold on her arm. She hit his chest, but he didn't seem to notice. "You really think you could kill our Hunters and get away with it?" he asked loudly with a tone that said how stupid such a thought had been.

I took a deep breath, then shouted, "I brought your daughter back to you. Let me go and no one gets hurt."

He laughed, a deep, dark sound. "One werewolf against seven armed Hunters? You're either an idiot or want to die."

I had to agree, but decided against saying so. I hit my head against the back of the jeep, cursing our naive belief that he would keep his word after all that had happened.

"Let him go, Dad. You promised," Nora shouted.

"I don't make promises with animals," her dad replied calmly.

"You promised me," she said. The scent of her fear and anger carried to me on the morning breeze. I worried that she would do something rash. "Let me go," she demanded. She raised her voice, "Vance, this was a mistake. This wasn't supposed to happen!"

"You're a fool for trusting a werewolf," her dad said in a tone heavily laced with disgust.

"I'm a fool for trusting you," she bit back.

He didn't respond. Instead, I heard the thud of several footsteps as his men moved to flank the jeep. I looked around for an escape, but found none.

"The men are in position, Rob."

"Good." He lifted his voice, "Fight and be shot again, or give up and come quietly," he said with an air that indicated he would rather shoot me again.

"Dad, no!" Nora protested. The sound of a struggle ensued followed by a sharp slap.

Nora sobbed softly and I longed to go to her, but knew any move in that direction would result in death. I kept a hand on my arm and reviewed my options.

Soft rustling came from the bushes lining the hill to my right and a slight fall of sand from the plateau on my left indicated that I was indeed surrounded. If the bullet in my arm was any indication, they were ordered to maim, not kill, which meant Rob planned on taking me in regardless of if I surrendered. None of the werewolves from Two knew I took Nora back to her father, so a rescue wouldn't come in time. Nora's attempts at dissuading her father from his plan were obviously in vain, and I didn't want to put her at risk for further injury.

I could choose to go with him and avoid more bullet holes which were swiftly becoming my least favorite thing, or I could wait for them to weaken me with silver bullets to the point that I wouldn't be able to defend myself. If the numbness in my arm was any indication, the bullets had been treated with the same coating that almost paralyzed me when Nora shot me at Two. Despite the instincts that demanded for me to fight back, I didn't stand a chance.

I took a deep breath, then stuck my hands out to the side of the jeep. "I'm coming out," I yelled.

"About time," Rob replied in a satisfied tone.

"No!" Nora protested, but she quickly fell silent.

I rose slowly and stepped into the open. Rob gave a minute motion with his hand. A bullet buzzed through the air and struck my thigh hard enough to knock me against the jeep. Pain flared through my leg.

"Dad, he gave up," Nora said with tears running down her cheeks.

"Just making sure," Rob replied. He nodded at his men and they advanced.

My instincts screamed for me to phase and fight, but my brain argued that my odds against seven loaded guns and apparently trigger-happy Hunters were slim. One man stepped forward and slapped a handcuff on one of my wrists, then jerked them roughly behind my back and fastened the other tight enough to cut into my skin. Blood trickled down my arm and dripped onto his sleeve. He looked at it in disgust, then wiped it on the front of my shirt before shoving me forward.

Nora shoved away from her father and ran across the pavement toward me. She hit the man on my right side across the jaw hard enough to rock him back, then followed it with a punch to the groin. He doubled over and she advanced toward the man on my left. He lifted his gun and took a step back, but glanced between Nora and her father and turned the gun on me instead.

"Run," Nora shouted, her voice full of pain at her father's betrayal.

Rob crossed the ground in massive strides and grabbed her upper arm in a tight grip that made her wince.

"Vance, I'm so sorry," she said, oblivious of the way her dad's fingers tightened until they turned white. "I didn't know, honest."

"I believe you," I said. Her eyes held mine, so green, sincere, and filled with such love it took my breath away. The man beside me shoved my shoulder directly on the bullet wound. I stumbled to the side, righted myself, and walked slowly to Rob's truck. Rob spoke to one of his men who then took Nora and led her to a car that appeared at the edge of the parking lot. I climbed inside the truck and watched her until she disappeared from view, convinced that it was the last time I would ever see her again.

# Chapter 11

"Wake up, mutt." The sneered words were followed by a kick to my ribs that awoke the pain in my side with a vengeance. My arms and legs were tied, which prevented me from defending myself against another kick. I winced and opened my eyes to see a white-walled room full of cages. "He's awake," the one who had kicked me said.

"Throw him in the cage," Rob's low voice answered.

Two men picked me up and threw me in a cage with bars on all sides and the bottom. My skin burned when I hit the floor. One of the men stepped in and cut the ropes with a quick slice of his knife, then slammed the cage door shut behind him. I stood shakily in an attempt to keep as little of my skin contacting the floor as possible. My bare feet seared where they touched the bars. I looked up to see Nora's father on the other side of the cage door, his arms crossed casually in front of his tailor-suited chest and his eyes boring into mine.

"Throw him a blanket," Rob said. His dark tone carried a hint of amusement at my pain.

A gray wool blanket that smelled of unwashed bodies landed in a heap at my feet. I stood on it, then met Rob's eyes again. "Where am I?" I demanded.

A humorless smile touched his lips. "The Werewolf Refinement Center, or Lobotraz, as we've come to call it thanks to the fact that no werewolf has ever escaped." He winked at one of the men next to him. "Alive, that is."

The three men chuckled and I wanted to smash their faces in as I had never wanted to hurt anyone before. I clenched my fists and pain ran up my arm where I had been shot. I glanced down to find a bandage over the wound. Another one had been wrapped around my thigh just below the tattered shorts I wore.

"Heal 'em to kill 'em," one of the other men said.

"Good thing they heal so quickly," Rob replied. He turned away, but said over his shoulder, "Makes torture that much more rewarding." They walked through the room and shut a large metal door at the end with a resounding clang.

I felt like I was going to vomit and sunk into a crouch on the blanket. I reached out a hand to steady myself, but stopped just before I grabbed the silver bars.

"Good move," a voice said from across the room.

I looked up to find another werewolf in a cage. Eight more cages lined that side of the wall and a glance to my right and left showed the same number on my side. Each cage contained a werewolf who watched me with mixed expressions of boredom, empathy, and anger.

"You want to touch the metal as little as possible. The coating absorbs in your skin and burns for hours," the werewolf concluded.

"Nice little trick he does with the blanket, too," the werewolf next to him agreed. He was seated on the floor of his cage, his blanket spread out to protect him from the bottom of his cell. "Waits until you burn your feet before he gives it to you. Likes to give you something to think about."

"Smarts, doesn't it?" a female voice asked next to me.

I turned see a girl a few years younger than me standing in the cell on my left. Mercifully, she had been given a tattered shirt to wear along with the unwashed ragged shorts that were the sole coverings of the other werewolves. She held something in her hand and lifted it for me to see. "It's just water," she explained, "but the more silver you wash off, the less it'll burn." She slipped her hand between the bars and waited for me to take the metal cup.

I took it, then winced as it burned my fingertips. "More silver, really?"

She shrugged. "They aren't very original. You get used to

it eventually; at least it hurts a little less."

"You shouldn't lie, Gem. Gives the new guys hope," the werewolf across from us admonished.

She rolled her eyes and gave me a winning smile. "Don't listen to them. I think they're starting to enjoy it here."

A cup flew across the aisle between us and hit Gem's cage with a loud crash. Everyone fell silent for a moment, but the door at the end of the room stayed closed.

"Smooth, Jake," Gem commented dryly. She turned back to me. "Use a corner of your blanket to wipe it off your feet; otherwise you'll be up all night with the pain."

"I don't think I'll be sleeping much," I said quietly, but I did as she instructed, and even though my feet still burned and angry red marks streaked across the bottoms where they had touched the bars, the pain lessened a bit.

Gem gave me a sad smile. "They're always the worst on the first day. You'll sleep, trust me."

"What are you talking about?" I pressed.

She toyed with the short strands of her blond hair which had once been trimmed into something resembling a pixie cut and refused to answer. I looked at the other werewolves. The one across from me cleared his throat. "I guess you'll find out soon enough." He rose and stretched in the confines of his cage. "They'll beat you until you phase, then whip you like a mangy cur with a silver cat-o-nine-tails that'll leave you as striped as a zebra."

He turned to demonstrate and a lump formed in my throat. Black marks that looked like charcoaled burns ran up and down his back. He flexed, then let out his breath slowly and turned back around.

"They healed like that?" I asked quietly.

He nodded. "They coat the whips with the same stuff as the bars. It burns and makes the healing process slower. And it never really stops hurting." He gave a grim smile. "They've got werewolf torture down to an art."

I dreaded the answer, but knew I had to ask. "What do they want?"

"The location of your pack." His even tone said that they had broken the information from him long ago. He met my eyes, his gaze grim and angry. "At least, that's what they tell you. Then, when you finally break and give it to them," his eyes narrowed and his expression left no room for argument, "And you will break."

The surety in his tone sent a cold chill down my spine.

He kept speaking, "Then even though they promised to kill you, they keep you here and torture you for the sheer, twisted pleasure of it. Day after day, month after month." His voice had risen to an angry shout.

He gripped the bars, ignoring the pain of the silver gel that covered them. "And there's no escaping it because our werewolf instinct doesn't let us kill ourselves and they won't kill us despite their promises!" A growl ripped from his throat and he hit his head against the bars so hard a trickle of blood ran down his forehead. He staggered back and sat down on his blanket. He touched the blood, then stared at his fingers as though he saw something within the dark red liquid.

"Don't mind Jake," Gem said quietly next to me. "He's been here a while."

"Everyone's been here a while," the werewolf in the cage next to Jake growled.

I ran a finger over the knuckles on my right hand and frowned. "What if you don't phase."

"They beat you to death," the werewolf on my other side answered. "But you'll phase. It's instinctual to protect ourselves and we can't fight it. It's their way of humiliating us after we've given in and told them what they want to know. They take away our humanity, forcing us to phase so they can beat us like dogs." He ran a hand through his dirty brown hair. "It's degrading."

"My friends will come for me," I said softly.

Jake lifted his bleeding head and laughed. Blood ran into his eyes, making him look even more deranged. "Your friends will come for you? Your pack?" He snorted. "Buried as deep as we are? You're as delusional as Gem."

Several of the other werewolves chuckled, the bitterness of their laughter as biting as it was haunting. I glanced at Gem. She shrugged. "My parents will come for me. I know they're searching. They'd never give up."

"Give it up, Gem," a female werewolf called from a few cages down. "After six months, I'd think you'd figure it out."

I stared at Gem. "You've been here six months? How old are you?"

"Sixteen," she replied. She gave a forced smile. "At least I don't have to worry about passing Driver's Ed."

"How did they find you?"

A cloud crossed her face. "I was at the movies with some friends. They jumped us when we were walking back to our car." She dropped her eyes, but I could still see the guilt in them. "They killed Kristy and Morgan when they found out they weren't werewolves." The tears in her voice betrayed the carefully emotionless expression on her face. "They'd still be alive if it wasn't for me."

"It's not your fault you're a werewolf," I pointed out. My heart ached for her pain. "Your parents would agree."

She gave me a sad smile. "I miss them."

"You'll see them again, don't worry." I met the eyes of the werewolf across the alley, daring him to disagree. "We'll get out of here." He snorted softly and turned around so his back was to us.

The door at the end of the room opened and four men walked in. "Gear up, newbie," the werewolf on my right whispered. "They're coming for you."

Their footsteps sounded loud in the cold gray room. Werewolves backed away from them and kept their eyes down as if afraid that eye contact would result in another beating. The men hit several of the cages as they passed, throwing taunting threats to the werewolves who cowered before them.

"Ready for another visit, mutt?" one asked, mocking a werewolf near the door.

"Miss me, sweetheart?" another said in a cruel tone that twisted in my gut as he hit a cage with his silver baton.

A guard hit Gem's cage and she met his eyes in a small act of defiance. He paused, his eyes glittering dangerously. "Looks like you need a little more attention," he said. "I'll make sure you get it."

The men stopped at my cage and a surge of adrenaline ran through my veins. I fought to keep from phasing to protect myself, pushing the instincts down with the threat of Jake's words lingering in the back of my mind. The men opened the cage door and motioned for me to come out. My feet burned when I walked across the bare bars, but I didn't let it show. One of the men shoved me and I stumbled, but I kept my footing and walked quietly with them past the cages of weary werewolves who watched me with mixed expressions of trepidation and sorrow.

One older woman in the cage nearest the door held the bars with age-spotted fingers. "Be strong," she whispered.

A guard hit her cage with a silver baton and she cowered against the back, but I met her eyes briefly and nodded before they shoved me through the door. The depth of pain, hunger, and hopelessness in her pale blue eyes haunted my soul.

\*\*\*

We made a very brief stop so I could relieve myself in a bucket in a corner while the guards turned their backs. I was informed that I would be given two such breaks a day, so to make them count. I was then led into a gray room where reinforced silver handcuffs were slapped around my wrists and looped across a cargo hook hanging from the ceiling. One of the guards that I recognized from the Four Corners meeting with Nora's dad pushed a button on a remote and the hook rose until my toes barely brushed the ground. The position made it hard to breathe and the ache in my side started to throb with my heartbeat.

"Think you could kidnap my daughter and not face the consequences?" Rob asked. He stepped into a view wearing a black tank-top and black pants that smelled of werewolf blood.

"Good to see you again," I said as pleasantly as I could muster.

He smiled, then punched me in the left side. I grimaced, but didn't give him the pleasure of hearing me yell. "It is pleasant to see me, isn't it?" he asked before punching me in the same place again.

I breathed out with the blow and concentrated on my heartbeat, willing my body not to phase and give in to the humiliation Jake spoke about. I refused to let them treat me like an animal, and the pride of the wolf in me agreed.

"A tough one, huh? Well, we have ways of breaking tough cases, don't we, Jeff?" Rob said. The guard with the button handed Rob a set of silver-plated gloves.

Rob pulled them on with a grim smile. "We have several preliminary questions to get out of the way. First, where's your pack? Nora's obviously been compromised by your lies and won't tell me, so it's up to you to give them up." He smiled when I didn't answer and punched me in the left side again.

Pain ran from my skin deep into my side and I gasped.

Rob gave a satisfied nod. "Hurts, doesn't it? The silver penetrates your natural defenses and allows you to feel the blows like an ordinary man. Convenient, isn't it?"

I held onto his statement that Nora wouldn't tell him the location of Two. The thought sent a surge of hope through my mind and also an echoing reminder of our kiss, the taste of her lips, and the heat of her hand against my chest.

The memory was shattered when Rob punched my right side with the silver-plated gloves. Pain exploded through my stomach and ribs with such force I couldn't hold in a yell of agony. The blow sucked the air from my body and zapped my strength so that I hung in the handcuffs with my toes brushing the ground.

When I met his eyes, Rob's eyebrows lifted. "You might be the biggest werewolf I've ever seen, but it seems even the giant has a weakness," he said. He punched the spot again and nodded when I yelled. He turned me on the chain and examined the scar on my right side. "What happened here?"

Fear of the pain and salvaging what was left of my pride made me speak. "I got it saving your daughter from a flash flood."

A flicker of emotion ran across his face and for one moment I thought he would be merciful, then his eyes hardened. "She left against orders, compromised herself, and cost me two-dozen Hunters in training. She would have deserved what she got." He punched my side again so hard black stars appeared in my vision and my thoughts grew hazy.

"Where's your pack?" he demanded.

He punched me again, tearing another yell from my unwilling lips, but I refused to answer.

"You will phase," he promised. "You'll tell me where you

pack is, then show me the color of your fur so I know what kind of a coward you are." He hit me again, but my body was growing numb and I merely gasped.

"Do you think he's an Alpha?" Jeff asked quietly from his side.

"There's only one way to find out," Rob replied grimly. He hit me again and when I didn't respond, he pulled me around to face him. "Phase," he shouted so loud my ears rang. I gave him a small smile and almost laughed at the anger that answered it. He hit me again and again, but I was the one in control and we both knew it.

"You don't want to phase? I'll live to make you regret it." Something hissed across the floor. I opened my eyes to see the nine whips of the cat-o-nine tails coated in silver. "You'll phase, or you'll die," Rob promised.

I closed my eyes and the sound of the whips through the air whistled loud in my ears before they bit into the skin of my back with a pain that sent electric shocks down my legs. I gritted my teeth so hard I was worried they would break, but an agonized yell betrayed me at the next lashing.

Rob whipped me until I no longer had the strength left to yell and I hung by my bleeding wrists, but I refused to phase. The grim pleasure I took in defying him was long gone, and I held onto my self-control because it was the last thing I had. His questions burned in my ears, but the answers to them had long fled my mind.

"Get him down," his deep, angry voice commanded.

The hook lowered with agonizing slowness until someone detached my handcuffs and I fell to the ground. Blood poured from the gashes across my back, but I couldn't feel them past the burning of the silver. I wondered vaguely if my back would heal striped like Jake's. It felt like a mess of raw hamburger meat.

"What should we do with the body?" Jeff didn't bother to

hide his disgust.

"Throw him in his cage. If he survives, we'll start over next time," came Rob's gruff response. A door slammed and his footsteps faded away.

I was dragged from the room by the handcuffs and vaguely aware of the cold tile floor of the werewolf room, a dim difference to the cold, porous cement in Rob's torture center. The guards grumbled about getting blood on themselves before they bent and chucked me heavily into the cage. The burn of the silver-coated bars under my skin felt like a lover's caress compared to the red, fiery pain of my back. I listened partially-conscious as the guards' footsteps left the room, returning it to the silence that had met our entrance.

"He didn't phase," Jake said from across the room. His statement carried such amazement and disbelief that if I could have found the strength to speak, I would have told him there was a point where phasing was the only thing Rob couldn't take from me. Through the pain, I would have told him the location of Two, of my parents, even of the dead Hunters' bodies, but the agony was so intense I couldn't even remember where they were. That I would have betrayed everyone burned in my heart with fierce shame.

"He must be an Alpha," Gem said quietly next to me. "Only an Alpha could have resisted, and even then, I've never seen it happen."

"They kill Alphas as soon as they find out that's what they are," the werewolf on my other side pointed out.

"Then maybe we're lucky he was strong enough not to phase," Gem concluded softly.

A hand touched my side, pulling down the blanket they had thrown over my back and shoulders to keep me from bleeding down the hallway as they dragged me.

"Oh my goodness," she said with a gasp.

"He'll bleed to death if those wounds don't heal," the woman further down replied.

"What do I do?" Gem asked with a tremor in her voice.

"Let me die," I forced out.

Her hand paused on my shoulder, then her voice strengthened and her touch was sure. "You're not dying if I can help it. You didn't give up in there, so you sure better not give up out here. I'm too young to watch my friends die."

"You know the wolves that never come back are dead, right?" Jake asked in a tone meant to be humorous.

"I've never watched them die," Gem shouted with a surge of anger that cut through the fog of my pain. "And I'm not about to," she concluded sharply with such agony in her voice that I was taken back to when I sat next to Nora in the shower, consoling her at the loss of her friends that I had helped kill.

They were both too young to see what they had seen. I would do whatever I could to lessen that. The irony that I wasn't much older than either of them sent a surge of determination through my body.

"It burns," I said softly through teeth clenched with the remaining strength I had.

"It's the silver," the woman down the row replied. "Gem, you've got to wash it out the best you can or his wounds will fester and never heal."

The sound of metal touching metal followed, then cold water was poured on my back. More water followed as werewolves passed their water rations through the bars to Gem's cage. The cold water eased the pain and the burning agony gave way to the relief of unconsciousness.

"Hang in there," Gem said before the black void took over.

# Chapter 12

I awoke slowly. Someone clanged on metal bars a few cages down, bringing back the harsh truth that what I had thought haunted me as a nightmare had been reality. I took a testing breath of heavy air tainted with blood, old sweat, and the scent of unwashed bodies and fear. The lash marks across my back throbbed, but with a healing ache. A knot formed in my stomach. I opened my eyes.

Gem smiled down at me from a few feet away. The bars between us didn't mar her cheerful countenance. "Hey there," she said, her blue eyes twinkling.

"Hey," I managed to get out. I pushed myself up slowly and noticed the brush of cloth against the wounds on my back. I glanced over my shoulder and saw that someone had torn a blanket into strips and used them to bind the lashes.

My heart slowed at the implication and I looked at Gem. She sat on the bars without anything to protect her from the harsh bite of the coated silver. I rose quickly to give her the blanket I had slept on. "You shouldn't have done that," I said before my knees weakened at the sudden movement and I had to catch myself against the bars.

Gem rose to help steady me, but wouldn't accept my blanket. "You needed it. It's alright."

I shook my head. "You didn't need to do that. It would have healed."

She gave a small shrug. "Maybe," she replied noncommittally. "You were bleeding pretty bad after all the silver washed out."

"But still." I couldn't fathom why she would do such a thing. I didn't know how long I had been out, but for every second of it some part of her had been touching the silver bars. The bottoms of my feet that contacted my own cage burned and I knew she hadn't spent the whole night on her feet. "Take it," I demanded.

She lifted an eyebrow at my tone and stepped back. She crossed her arms on her chest and tipped her head to one side tauntingly. "You gonna make me?"

I let out a frustrated breath. "If I have to, yes." I threw the blanket into her cell, then took one of the cloths from my back, tore it into two, and bound my feet so that they didn't have to touch the bars.

Gem watched me for a minute and I could tell she wanted to argue, but I stared her down until her werewolf instincts wouldn't let her argue. "Fine," she muttered. She turned to pick it up and my stomach dropped at the angry red burns that ran in lines across her legs where her pants were too short to cover them.

"You shouldn't have done that," I whispered again, sick at the thought that she had suffered for me.

She spread the blanket on the floor of her cell as if she hadn't heard me, then sat in the middle facing me like a girl in a field of flowers. "Happy?" she asked.

I rubbed my eyes and crouched to slow the dizziness that swam through my head. I reached out to steady myself against the bars, and remembered where I was at the last minute. I took another of the cloths from my back, tore it into two, then wrapped it around my hands. "I'm not happy that you got hurt helping me," I said.

She shrugged and I saw burn marks on her arms where she had touched the bars when she tended my wounds. She noticed me looking and folded her arms again. "I was in better shape to take it than you were," she said with a slight touch of defiance. Then she gave another cheerful smile. "And you're better now, so it was all worth it."

I wasn't so sure, but I didn't want to make her sacrifice seem less. I used the rest of the strips of cloth to wrap a few bars in a corner so I could sit down. I eased to a sitting position and glanced around. Jake met my eyes from across the aisle, then dropped his gaze.

"You're an Alpha, aren't you?" he asked sullenly.

"Does it matter?" I questioned, curious.

His eyebrows rose and he looked just to the right of my face. "You're kidding, right? Rob and the other extremist Hunters thrive on finding and destroying Alphas. Apparently it's their life goal."

The term caught my attention. "Extremist Hunters? I thought all Hunters killed werewolves."

The werewolf on my right side rose to his knees. "Thanks to Jaze, most Hunters work with werewolves now instead of hunting us. He created peace between the races and saved numerous lives, included my family." He gave me a look of disbelief. "You haven't heard of him?"

I shook my head. "I've been a bit distant from werewolf news," I said, unwilling to divulge more than that. "Tell me about him."

The others listened in with the attention of pained souls looking for any distraction. The werewolf thought for a minute, then let out a breath. "He has a team of Alphas and grays that works better than any pack I've ever seen. They're like S.W.A.T., but for werewolves. They save troubled werewolves from situations like fighting rings, hostile neighbors, and territory problems. They've helped relocate thousands of families after Jaze's uncle tried to wipe out all of the Alphas."

"His uncle?" I asked to be sure. I wondered if it was the same werewolf who made my parents keep me in hiding at Two. So many Alphas were killed, the purity of Alpha blood barely survived.

The werewolf nodded. "His uncle killed Jaze's father and nearly succeeded in taking him down as well. We're lucky he was smarter as well as stronger."

"I've always wanted to meet him," the older werewolf near the door said. Her voice shook slightly. "He rescued two of my boys from a fighting ring and brought them back to me."

"A guardian of werewolves," I said with a touch of humor. The thought made me smile with the absurdity of it.

The werewolf who first spoke glared at me. "Yes, a guardian of werewolves," he said in a growl that begged me to smile again.

I held up a hand, lacking the strength to defend myself against his rage at the moment. "Alright, I'm sorry. So what's keeping Jaze from finding this place?"

"He'll find it," Gem said with stark certainty. I glanced at her and she grinned. "If anyone can find Lobotraz, he can."

"Since your parents aren't having any success," a werewolf a few cages down muttered.

I changed to the subject to distract her. "Lobotraz. Who came up with that stupid name?"

She laughed, the sound bright amid the grays that filled the room. "Rob, I guess. He likes the way it rolls dramatically off his tongue."

I chuckled, then held my side. "Tell me about the extremists and why they're still around if Jaze united the Hunters and werewolves."

"Not all Hunters were eager to resolve concerns, as you can imagine," the werewolf next to me answered. "But the extremists are worse than the Hunters ever were. They're cruel as well as vigilant. I've never seen anything like it."

"Tell me about it," another werewolf said from further down. "They burned my house with my family in it while they made me watch. Luckily I made an escape passage they didn't know about or my children would be dead. They got away." He sighed. "At least I think they did."

The door at the end of the room opened and two women

118

dressed in tattered blue clothes came in. The first carried bowls and the other ladled foul-smelling food into each one before shoving it under the small gap at the bottom of the cell door. The werewolves closest to the door ate their food hastily, but the further down they went, the slower the werewolves ate. At my questioning look, Gem gave a sad smile.

"Beating day comes once a week. Those closest to the door are first. If they don't eat quickly, their food is taken away when they're beaten." The resigned note in her voice warred with the forced cheerful smile on her face. I know I didn't imagine the glint of fear in her eyes at the coming beating.

"This can't go on forever. Someone's going to find us," I said with a surety.

Jake let out a growl. "Don't fill her head full of hope. Look where that's gotten all of us. Forever is a long time when you're subjected to the whims of people like Rob and his men. They've given a new meaning to cruel and unusual punishment."

"Punishment for being a werewolf." The werewolf next to me let out a deep, humorless laugh. "We aren't the first race hated for what we were born being, and we won't be the last."

"That doesn't make it right, Rex," Gem replied calmly as though they had argued the issue many times.

The women slid a bowl under my door and my stomach turned at the scent that wafted from it.

"Pretend it's beef broth with bread crumbs," Gem whispered. She hunched over her soup with her eyes closed.

"What is it really?" I asked.

"Probably whatever scraps he finds from the slaughterhouse down the road. They get pretty inventive with the ingredients," Rex replied. He grabbed his bowl when it cleared the door and slurped down the contents without pause. He threw the bowl down and looked like he was going to throw it all back up, but he took several breaths, then gave me a triumphant look. "That's how it's done."

"Lovely," I muttered under my breath. I took a few quick swallows of the foul-smelling stuff, then my stomach brought it back up and I retched in the corner.

Several werewolves protested, but Gem gave me a sympathetic smile. "Don't worry. The hungrier you get, the better it tastes." She sipped hers delicately as though it truly was beef broth.

My stomach growled, but I couldn't bring myself to even look at the soupy mixture again, let alone drink it. I sighed and lifted it towards Gem. "Want it?" She hesitated, but I could see the hunger in her eyes. "I'm not going to finish it, and you might as well eat it now before it turns into an even more delectable delicacy."

I passed it through the bars and she took the bowl with both hands. She studied me for a second, then downed the soupy mixture quickly. She used a finger to clean the remaining glop from the edges and threw me a grateful smile. "I don't remember the last time I was full."

"When we get out of here, I'll make sure you're never hungry again," I promised.

Several angry mutters rose from around the room, but I was surprised that Jake kept quiet. I glanced his way and found him watching me, a look of approval on his face. At my questioning look, he nodded his head toward Gem's two empty bowls. I gave a small smile and settled back on the hard bars.

The door opened and the older female werewolf who had told me to stay strong cowered against the back of her cage. The guards hauled her out and forced her through the door, then grabbed the male werewolf in the cage across from her.

"They beat two at a time?" I asked quietly.

Gem shook her head. "They usually take their time with us unless they're saving it for someone in particular." Her eyes met mine and they widened. She looked across at Jake, her expression pleading. "They're not going to take him again, are they?"

A surge of fear ran through me at the thought of the whips and silver gloves. I didn't know if I could take such a beating again, but I tried not to let the fear show.

"It's hard to say," Jake replied, his tone truly bothered. "But Rob definitely has a burr under his skin."

The werewolves were returned about an hour later. Both had phased to wolf form and bloody lines traced through their tattered hides. They were thrown back into the cages where they limped to their blankets and tried to sleep off the worst of the pain. The guards moved to the next two wolves and the process began again.

Gem didn't cower when they reached her. She held her head high and gave me a brief, courageous smile before they pulled her from the cage.

"Leave her alone," Jake yelled from across the way. "She's just a kid. You are all savages!"

The guards ignored him and took the werewolf across from her. They forced them down the aisle and out of the room. After what felt like hours later, they brought Gem back in wolf form, her cream-colored fur striped in red. She met my eyes briefly; her blue gaze was filled with pain and humiliation before she ducked her head and hunched on the blanket in the corner. The guards tossed in her tattered clothes, then slammed the cage door.

She winced at the sound and I hated them more than anything for hurting her and making her so afraid. I wanted to tear the guards from limb to limb and had to fight to keep from phasing. Jake's words echoed in my head, warning me that they would destroy an Alpha as soon as he manifested. If there was ever a chance to escape, I had to keep my wits about me because it was the only way I could save Gem from this fate worse than death.

The guards skipped my cage and finished with the rest of the werewolves, fifteen in all. When the last pair were thrown back into their cages, Jeff opened the door and walked down to stop in front of mine. A taunting smile touched his face. "Rob wants to see you, mutt."

I checked the watch I didn't have and shook my head. "Sorry, he's too late. All of my appointments are filled for the day."

Jeff looked like he wanted to rip my head off. He motioned to the two guards. "Get him out of there."

When they entered my cell, I fought back the urge to phase and teach them all a lesson. I knew my life and possibly the lives of those in the other cells depended on me keeping my Alpha heritage a secret as long as possible. If I could hold out until a rescue came, I would be in a position to deal much greater damage to Rob's Lobotraz. I walked with them up the row and tried to shut out the scent of fresh blood and fear that came from the cages I passed.

"What a coincidence that Row Four's interrogation day came the day after your initiatory beating," Rob said in a tone that indicated there was no such thing as a coincidence at Lobotraz.

"It's wonderful," I replied dryly. Pain tore through the healing wounds along my back and the bruises on my ribs and stomach when Jeff attached my handcuffs to the hook. I was pulled up again so my feet barely touched the floor.

Rob walked around me slowly, a hand on his jaw. He nodded when he reached the front of me again. "Looks like you're actually healing quite well." A gleam came to his eyes. "I suppose we'll have to do all we can to make sure you're the least comfortable before you phase or die." His eyebrow rose thoughtfully. "Of course, I have a suspicion that phasing and dying will occur at the same time. My daughter won't confess as to your coat color, but I'll take a stab that a werewolf who would stand against his pack for a human would have to be an Alpha or they'd tear him apart. It seems you animals can't attack your superiors."

The fact that he was still trying and failing to get information from Nora lifted my heart. I met Rob's eyes, my own defiant. "You humans have to chain and handcuff your superiors before you attack them."

Surprise quickly turned to rage on his face when my insinuation registered. He reached for the cat-o-nine-tails and backed up so that he faced me squarely. "Let's make the chest match the back, shall we?"

\*\*\*

The skin across my chest and stomach stood in tatters by the time they threw me back in my cage. Every breath hurt. I pulled into a fetal position on the rag-covered bars in the corner and willed my heart to keep pumping. Blood dripped through the bars to the dirty cement below, forming dark puddles that covered the prior stains and creating a soft patter that sounded loud in the quiet room.

I closed my eyes and listened to my heart beat and the flow of air through my wheezing lungs. An edge of one of the whips had sliced along my ribs like a fillet knife, leaving a wound clear to the bone on my right side. The pain mixed with the wound that refused to heal in the same side was so intense I could barely breathe.

"You alright?" Gem asked softly.

A wry chuckle escaped my lips and I winced at the pain it brought. "Just peachy," I said without moving.

"That's what I thought. Here."

It took me several minutes to will my body to respond. When I finally lifted my head, I found that Gem and the other werewolves had phased back to human form and pulled on their clothes. Most of the werewolves looked like they were starting to heal, which made me wonder how long I had been with Rob.

"We didn't think you were coming back," Gem said in a voice that quavered slightly with suppressed emotion.

I pushed up to my hands and knees, but a wracking cough tore through my lungs and had me hunched over in pain for several more minutes. When I could finally breathe again, I wiped the blood from my mouth and gave her a half-hearted smile. "You know I'm harder to kill than that."

"You've got to be an Alpha," Jake said. "Otherwise he wouldn't hate you so much." Jake had torn a piece of his blanket off and wrapped it around half of his face. It looked like one of the whips had caught him in the eye when he was a wolf. I couldn't tell if he would be able to see out of it again.

I let out a steadying breath and sat up gingerly. Gem handed me a cup of water and I used it to wash out the worst of the wounds. "He's got plenty of reasons to hate me; at least he thinks so." I met Gem's searching gaze. "I might have saved his daughter's life on more than one occasion."

She smiled in understanding. "Nora."

My eyes widened in surprise even as my heart leaped at the images her name brought. "Yes. How do you know her name?"

"You say it in your sleep. You whispered her name over and over again yesterday when I couldn't tell if you were going to live or die." She sighed and leaned her back against the bars, then winced and sat up. "Tell us about her."

"I shouldn't." I didn't know if I could put the last few days into words, and didn't want to bring worse punishment down on any of them by telling them things Rob didn't want told. But the thought that Rob would want it kept a secret spurred me on.

I told them about the attack on Two and stopping Drake and Seth before they could kill her. They laughed when I told how she shot me, then removed the bullet. I told them about the hike and finding the missing hikers, then the full moon and jumping into the ravine before she could be swept over the cliff.

Everyone kept silent when I told them about the kiss, surprising myself as much as them with the admittance. When I told them about Rob's promise of safety and my own naivety in believing he would actually uphold his word, several of them laughed, but they were laughs tinged with bitterness at the outcome instead of making fun of my costly mistake.

"You love her, don't you?" Gem asked after I stopped talking.

The words brushed my heart like the softest kiss and I sighed. "I do," I admitted. "We haven't known each other for very long, but I felt from the first moment I saw her that there was something there."

"You're a romantic," the older female werewolf by the door said quietly.

"You're a fool," Jake echoed.

I shrugged, then brought my knees up and leaned my head on them in an effort to ease the strain on my damaged chest. "Either way, it's a lost cause."

"You're getting out of here," Gem said firmly.

I gave her a slight smile. "Regardless, I doubt I'll ever see her again. She's the daughter of a Hunter who wants to kill me more than anything, but can't quite bring himself to do it. He wants to break me first, to make me beg. I worry that he'll bring Nora into it if I don't give in."

"He wouldn't dare," Gem breathed. "His own daughter?"

"Not like he's shown any scruples up to this point," Rex pointed out.

I breathed out slowly and told myself he wouldn't go so far, but the doubt in my mind scared me more than his silver whip.

# Chapter 13

I awoke that night to the sound of a whimper, and looked over to see Gem roll over in her sleep, one arm stretched along the silver-coated bars. I sat up and wrapped a cloth around my arm, then stuck it through the cage and moved her arm gently back to her side so it wouldn't get burned. She opened her eyes and looked at me with the bare gaze of someone whose walls had been lowered by sleep.

I saw a scared girl who was afraid she had been forgotten and left to die despite the brave front she put on for the others. The pain she felt at the lashes along her back burned in her blue gaze, and the hopelessness that reflected back at me made my heart ache. I reached my hand back through and she grabbed it as though it was a life-line.

"We're going to make it through this," I breathed softly, wary about waking up the others.

"I don't know how much longer I can last," she said, her lips barely moving. She took a breath and winced at the way it pulled at the healing lashes along her back.

"You'll outlast every werewolf here," I said. Sadness swept through her gaze and I realized she took my words wrong. I tightened my grip on her hand. "You're the bravest, strongest person I've ever met. You've got to survive because you're pulling every other wolf here through. They're all counting on you to make it."

She closed her eyes and opened them again wet with tears that she refused to let spill over. "I won't let them down," she said, an edge of determination to her soft voice.

I nodded and moved closer to the bars so that I could sleep with my hand holding hers. The simple touch of our fingers was so pure and innocent amid the scent of blood and decay, pain and unwashed bodies. Neither of us wanted to let go.

***

By the beatings, I had been in Lobotraz for three mind-numbing weeks. Jake and then the older woman by the door failed to come back from interrogations a week ago, and their cages remained bare reminders of the lives they once held. I took heart in the fact that no other werewolves replaced them, but between the beatings, the poor quality of food, and the inhumane living conditions, hope was fading quickly. Gem kept up her tirade abut her parents coming to save her, but the lack of response from Two nearly broke my heart.

The skin of my chest and back was covered in blackened scars from the whips. My side still ached and Rob favored the spot during his interrogations. Tomorrow night was the full moon, and I knew if I refrained from phasing during today's beating, I wouldn't be able to hide the fact that I was an Alpha after nightfall.

The next round of interrogations started and I waited in numb silence as each cage was emptied and then rejoined by a beaten wolf whose eyes shone with less life than before. Gem had been taken and it barely registered to me that the guards came to get me before she was thrown back in. Two forms dressed in black stopped in front of my cage. I rose stiffly to my feet and waited for them to enter. My mind screamed for me to attack them, to overthrow everyone at Lobotraz regardless of the fact that I would be sorely outnumbered and weaponless even if I enlisted the help of the other half-starved, weak werewolves who would get themselves killed.

I toyed with the idea that being killed was far better than being a prisoner at Rob's whim when an achingly familiar smell touched my nose. One of the guards slapped on my handcuffs and I noticed there was no pain. I glanced down to find that the cuffs weren't silver.

"Play along," the guard whispered. I looked at him closely, but there was nothing I recognized about his dark blond hair and brown eyes.

I was about to question him when he held up something. My heart slowed at Nora's scent covering the scarf he drew from his pocket. "You're Vance, right?" he whispered. At my shocked nod, he tipped his head. "Then let's get you out of here. Unless, of course, you want to stay and get tortured. I hear you're next in line."

I shook my head, then met Rex's wide eyes from the next cage. "What about the others?" My heart balked. "We have to wait for Gem. We can't leave any of them."

The pretend guard grabbed my arm in a grip I couldn't break. I realized with a start that he was also a werewolf, and probably an Alpha by his strength. His companion, a black-haired werewolf with dark blue eyes, watched me warily as though he was prepared to take me down at any sign of a struggle.

"I'm Jaze," the werewolf who gripped my arm said. The werewolves in the cages around me stirred at the name and I stared at him. He looked at the others. "I promise I'll come back for each of you. Stay strong. You won't have to wait long for a rescue." It was obvious by the tone of his voice that he didn't want to leave any werewolf in such horrible conditions, but he had no choice. He lowered his voice, "But we've got to go now or we lose our window," he told me in a firm undertone. "We can't wait for anyone, but I promise we'll return soon for the others."

Two more werewolves appeared at his shoulder. One had dark red eyes that studied me while he listened to someone speak into his earpiece. "We've got to go now," he told Jaze quietly.

Jaze stepped back and I moved to follow, but the thought of Gem returning to her life in the cage and of the other

CHEREE ALSOP

werewolves being punished just for being born pounded in my mind. I couldn't step past the cage opening. I grabbed onto the bars and resisted despite the way they burned my hands.

"Oh, for heaven's sake," the black-haired werewolf said. He raised something and smashed it against the side of my head. I fell in a heap to the ground and the world closed over me.

# Chapter 14

"How long do you think he'll sleep?" Nora's worried voice pierced my floating thoughts.

"I'm not sure," Jaze replied. "He's been through a lot. The conditions were worse than we feared. My team is working on a strategy so we can rescue the others."

A soft hand touched my head. "I wish he would have come out willingly."

"Me, too," Jaze replied in a tone laced with regret. "Jet didn't want to hit him, but he put up a struggle at leaving the rest of the werewolves."

"That's Vance," Nora said with such aching familiarity the last hold of unconsciousness drifted away. I opened my eyes to see the blond-haired werewolf sitting on a chair next to Nora. His black-haired friend, Jet, leaned against the door jamb with his arms crossed. His eyes flicked to mine and he eased to a standing position. Nora blinked and tears shone in her eyes. "I can't believe my father did this. I didn't want Vance to get hurt. It's all my fault. I hate the thought of other werewolves experiencing what he did."

Jaze's voice was touched with understanding, "I wouldn't have left them, but I couldn't risk my team to get anyone else out. We risked more than our lives going down there. If we were caught-"

"What?" Nora asked when he stopped talking.

He glanced at his friend, then followed his gaze to me. "Well, looks like we got him out alive after all." He gave me a friendly smile and motioned for Nora to turn around.

Nora stood and the tears that had pooled in her eyes overflowed. She knelt by my side. Her hands hovered over me for a moment as though she wanted to hug me but didn't know how to do so without hurting me. She settled for taking one of my hands. "You're awake, and you're here. I can't believe you're here." Her tears ran down her cheeks and fell on my hand.

I rose on my elbows and kissed her; she started in surprise, then returned the kiss with a longing and relief my soul echoed. "I missed you," I said when I finally pulled back.

She stared at me as though she didn't know what to say. "I'm so sorry," she began, but I cut her off.

"Don't apologize. I know you had nothing to do with it. Believe me, your father cleared that up many times." I sat up gingerly and she rose anxiously as though she should help but didn't know how. I took her hand and held it. "I'm alright." Her eyes ran over the charred, healed skin that striped my chest. I took her chin gently in my free hand and moved her eyes to meet mine. "It's not as bad as it looks, trust me. I don't really have much pain right now except for a splitting headache." I shot Jet a glance and he met my gaze directly. Surety of his own strength wafted from him and I knew he had to be another Alpha by his unflinching manner. Alphas were scarce. Besides being at Two, it was strange to find even this many working together.

"It could have gone smoother," Jaze replied. "We didn't plan on having to knock you out to get you out of there."

My heart clenched at the thought of the werewolves I had left behind. "We've got to rescue them." I glanced around and found that we were in a small room in a house that smelled of werewolves, humans, and the unmistakable odor of gunpowder and iron. By the scent of other werewolves who had stayed in the room for short periods of time, I guessed we were in one of Jaze's safe houses. It felt surreal and wrong to be safe when the others were still trapped at Lobotraz. I rose from the bed and stood a moment to let the brief dizziness pass.

"Where are you going?" Nora asked.

"I can't relax here while they're suffering."

Jaze blocked my path and when I moved to walk past him, he put a hand on my chest. "You're not in any shape to help anyone," he pointed out.

At my look, he dropped his hand, but didn't move out of the way. "I'm in better shape then they are. I can't leave them there!"

His eyes met mine with sympathy. "I understand what you're going through, trust me. Freeing werewolves and helping them return to their homes is what I do." His gaze darkened. "We've been searching for the entrance to Lobotraz for months. When Nora contacted us, she made us agree to look for you immediately if she gave us the info we were lacking. We upheld our end of the agreement, but also found out how under prepared we were to storm the place."

"That doesn't matter," I said stubbornly. I heard myself, but the image of Gem hunched in a dark corner in pain after pointless interrogations refused to leave my mind. Nora's hand slipped into mine and I longed for a brief moment that it was Gem's. The thought surprised me.

"It does." Jaze frowned slightly, his brown eyes dark. "I'm not going to risk my pack or our support if we can get through this without putting lives in danger."

"Lives are already in danger," I said quietly.

"And we're preparing to rescue them. I need you to trust me and give me the time I need to gather additional information."

He held my eyes until I finally nodded. It wasn't until he turned away that I noticed Jet had fallen silently back to my left side to easily defend Jaze if I became a threat.

The red-eyed werewolf came to the door. "Jaze, there's a problem with Jerome's pack. He's wondering if he could speak to you."

Jaze nodded and glanced at me as if he wanted to say something, then he gave me a smile and turned away. I

133

watched until they left through the door and closed it behind them, then I sank onto the bed and buried my head in my hands.

"We'll go back," Nora promised softly. She brushed my unruly hair from my face with gentle fingers. "We've got to stop my dad."

"He's a cruel man," I replied quietly.

Her fingers traced one of the many black scars across my back. "Did he do this to you?" Her voice carried pain at the thought, but also defiance as though she needed to know.

I nodded without speaking. She put her forehead against my back and I relished the touch of her breath against my bare skin. "I can't let him do it to others."

"I know," she breathed. "I feel the same way."

The touch of her hand against my skin brought back memories of Gem's small hand held in mine, my arm wrapped in tattered cloths to prevent it from being burned by the silver bars. The thought of holding her hand each night had kept me going. I felt like I betrayed her now, feeling Nora's reassuring touch while she was still beaten and tortured. One part of my heart ached for that hand in mine again. The feelings warred against each other, confusing my motivations and what I thought I knew about myself. I shoved the emotions deep down and allowed myself for that instant to just be safe.

We sat in silence for several moments and I pushed away all feelings of guilt, the lingering pain that never left my scars and the ache in my side, and the fear of what was happening to Gem. I took a deep breath and lived just for the brush of Nora's lips against my back, the way her long black hair tickled my skin, the subtle scent of vanilla and sunflowers that complemented her spring green eyes. The fact that I was surrounded by her scent made it feel real, like I was home. Except my home had let me down.

The moment of no regrets faded at the thought of Two. "Where're the werewolves from Two? Did you talk to them when I was taken?"

She was silent so long I sat up and turned to face her. A pit formed in my stomach at the look on her face. She stared at me for a minute, then shook her head and dropped her eyes. "I tried, but they gave up when they couldn't find you."

I forced my voice to remain steady. "They gave up," I repeated in a neutral tone. "How long did they look?"

"A week," Nora said so softly I could barely hear her. "When they gave up, I went looking for Jaze."

Rage filled my veins. I pictured myself two weeks ago at the time they stopped looking, beaten, starving, and still hanging onto the hope that they would come. I had given them everything, safety, a life of freedom, education, training, security, camaraderie, and a group of friends to act as a pack, and in return they couldn't bother themselves to look longer than the length of a spring vacation for the one who had given them their world.

I pushed up from the bed.

"Where are you going?" Nora asked.

"Two. I have some things to take care of."

Her hand slipped into mine. "We'll go together."

I wanted to argue, but her fingers felt so good entwined with mine that I merely nodded and led the way.

***

The hurt and rage that started at Jaze's safe house built during the long drive. When we reached the bottom of the red rocks and the trail that branched away hidden from view behind an outcropping, my emotions were a solid knot of fury. The new hiking boots and clothes I wore felt stiff and rough against my healing skin. Nora walked beside me with the determined step of an angry woman, each stride sending up small puffs of sand from her black boots. I knew the werewolves at Two should fear her as much as me.

Drake was on sentry duty and let out a yell when he saw us. He ran down the rocks, took one look at the anger I could barely contain, and rushed ahead of us to the caves.

I wasn't surprised to see Brian and Ben waiting beside Thomas at the door. Traer stood in the background, and the relief in his eyes was so stark when he saw me that it almost buckled my resolution, but the sight of the two Alphas I had kicked out standing at my door so smug as though they owned the place brought it all back. They stepped into the room when I entered, but didn't give way more than that.

"You gave up after a week?" I shouted, too angry to bother lowering my voice.

"We looked," Thomas said. "We just didn't know where to start."

"For *one week*?" I demanded. "Really?"

Brian stepped forward. "That's what you deserve for putting Two in danger."

Red flashed before my eyes. "Two is mine!" I reminded them with a growl so menacing Brian bared his teeth. "It was built with my family's money and we've allowed you to stay here to save your lives." I stared at him, my chest heaving and so much rage in my heart I couldn't voice the rest of my thoughts.

"For no reason," Brian shot back. "Alphas aren't being killed off like they were. There are wolves living normal lives without having to cower in some cave hideout."

"Then why are you here?" I growled.

Ben met my eyes, his own filled with defiance and self-righteousness. "Because with you gone, Two needed a new leader."

"Thought waiting a month was long enough before replacing me?" I asked, loathing thick in my voice.

Ben's gaze turned smug. "We only waited a week."

"Until you verified that I was nowhere to be found and hopefully wasn't coming back." My limbs shook with the urge to phase, but there was one more thing I needed to know. I met Traer's gaze across the room and couldn't hide the pain in my voice. "Where were you?"

He dropped his eyes, the regret in them so deep I already knew the answer.

I took a step toward him. "You couldn't defy the Alphas long enough to even search for me?" My voice lowered. "You were my best friend," I forced out just above a whisper.

The lack of denial hurt worse than any of Rob's tortures. The Alpha in me did the only thing it could with the pain; it turned it into a blind, red rage.

I phased so fast nobody had time to react. I leaped out of my ruined clothes straight at Brian. He fell over backwards with my fangs sunk deep into his arm.

"Let him go!" Ben yelled. Something hit me on the back, but I barely felt it. I spun and grabbed him by the knee, then pulled him down on top of his brother.

Thomas had already phased when I glanced to make sure he wasn't going to attack my back. The Alpha met my gaze calmly, then he turned and trotted out of Two. My eyes drifted to Traer who cowered back against the wall, his hands closed into helpless fists and a look on his face as though he wanted to sink into the red rock wall behind him and never be seen again. When our eyes met, he mouthed, "I'm sorry," but it was too little, too late.

Sharp teeth grabbed my back leg. I turned and caught Brian by the back of the neck before he could bite down. He froze at the pressure of my teeth on his spine. His muscles twitched in my jaws and I wanted to clamp down so badly my bones ached. I wanted them to see what Rob and Lobotraz had done to me, to feel my pain and to recognize utter hopelessness. I wanted them to suffer the way I had.

I closed my eyes as the thought surfaced that the feelings weren't really me. I wanted revenge, but Brian and Ben were acting like Alphas fighting for territory. They might have been happy that I was gone, but I couldn't deny the relief I had felt when I first chased them out of Two.

I let Brian go and waited for him to scramble back to his brother's side. Both Alphas watched me, unsure of what to do. The fact that there was even a question brought another vehement snarl from my chest. I ran at them and they both darted past Nora and out the door.

I turned back to find Traer in his wolf form, his gray coat blending with the shadows. Of any of them, his betrayal hurt the worst. I bared my teeth and gave a long, low growl that reverberated through the room. Traer ducked his head and padded slowly past. I listened to his footsteps until they faded away.

I left Nora in the main room and stalked to my quarters. I phased, pulled on some clothes, glanced once at the phone filled with thirty messages, no doubt from my worried mother, then turned and left without taking anything. I found the gas cans in the rec room and took the propane from the kitchen. I dumped gasoline in the various rooms, a cool, collected fury fueling my actions.

At one point, Drake and Max walked in on me.

"What are you doing?" Drake demanded.

I turned on him with a growl that would have rivaled my rage as a wolf. "Get out and never come back." Drake put up his hands and backed away.

Max stayed in the doorway, his eyes on the gasoline container in my hands. "You need to think this through," he said. "You don't realize what you're doing."

I threw the container so hard it smashed against the wall next to him and flooded the room with the scent of gasoline. "For the first time in my life," I said in a voice fueled by heartache and pain, "I truly realize what I'm doing."

His face washed pale at the cold anger in my voice and he turned and left without a word; by the time I made it back to Nora, the other werewolves had heard of my rage and vacated Two.

Nora watched silently when I struck a match and tossed it into the main living room. She followed me out the door and I led us to a rock ledge a few hundred yards back. Nora ducked behind it and I stood on top.

My heart exploded with the propane canisters, sending yellow and blue flames out the door and above Two where the ceilings had once been lined with glass to let in the most light. The anger and betrayal I felt matched the fury of the flames. I took a deep breath and yelled in a furious, wordless cry all of the hatred and hopelessness I had experienced at Rob's hands, the loss of my friends and camaraderie at Two, and the frustration that Gem and the other werewolves at Lobotraz were suffering because of who they were.

The yell cleared my rage and left me empty and ragged. I wanted more than anything to be out of anyone's sight, to be alone with the pain of betrayal and to forget what Two had once stood for.

"I'll be back," I said shortly to Nora. She nodded with a

look of understanding and I left her at the inferno that was once the entrance to Two.

# Chapter 15

The sunset was darker than usual, reds and golds colored deep with the smoke from my home. I closed my eyes and memories flashed by, images of happier times, young boys learning to cook with instructions from the internet, the numerous challenges we gave each other every day in the training room, and playing soccer, frisbee, and football in the expansive desert that we used as a stadium.

A knot formed in my throat at a memory of Sam days after he had arrived. His parents shipped him in at my mother's recommendation, and the young boy became my shadow for the next year. He viewed everything I did with wide, awe-filled eyes and the hope that one day he would be as strong as me despite being a gray coat. I supported his dreams of becoming a doctor like Traer, the friend who refused to search for me because of Brian and Ben.

Traer used to treat the Alphas as distant superiors despite the fact that he and I were only a few days apart in age. But then I was bit by a rattlesnake while making rounds. I didn't return at my scheduled time, and while the others laughed it off, Traer searched for me. I was still in wolf form because I worried that phasing would send the venom more quickly through my veins, and when he found me, my back leg where I had been bitten was so swollen I could barely move it.

Traer carried me over four miles back to Two and treated me through the fever delirium. He kept his promise not to tell my parents what had happened because I foolishly worried that they would take me from Two and not let me come back. Later on, Ben challenged him for his devotion to me and would have beaten him to a pulp as an example to the others, but I happened to walk in on the first punch and gave both Brian and Ben such a beating that they hadn't challenged me again until the attack a month ago.

The fire tinted the twilight sky in red, lapping flames that died until only charcoal and seared red rock were left. I lost myself staring into the burning embers; an echo of pain ached in the charred scars along my body. I wondered if Two could possibly feel the same loss of humanity.

I had a mild regret that Gem hadn't seen Two before I destroyed it. On long nights at Lobotraz, I told her of the werewolves who lived there and our adventures and pitfalls. She would have liked the sunlight filtering down to the marble floors and the way the red particles smelled of dusty cinnamon as they floated through the air trapped in beams of light. Thoughts of the werewolf confused me. I felt so at home with Nora, like I was complete, but my mind and soul still longed after Gem as though a werewolf was a better match for me, a soul mate. Now that I had Nora back, I worried that I couldn't appreciate her because I longed for Gem's hand in mine again.

Soft footsteps made their way up to my viewing point, erasing my fears. Just the promise of Nora's company stilled my emotions and cleared my troubled heart. I took a breath of the breeze that brought her scent.

"You don't have to be alone up here," she said quietly, stopping a few feet back to give me my space.

I didn't trust the emotions that ran across my face at the sound of her voice and turned slowly, hoping the darkness hid what I couldn't. "You weren't part of this. I shouldn't have let you come."

"I wanted to," she replied.

I tipped my head toward the light that touched the darkening horizon. "It's a full moon. I don't want to leave you alone."

A smile touched her shadowed lips. "I haven't felt alone since I met you." The smile fell and her lip quivered slightly before she bit it. She turned away and I could smell her regret on the evening breeze. "It's my fault," she said so quietly I barely heard her.

I shook my head. "You had nothing to do with it."

She met my gaze, defiance and pain in her eyes. "You wouldn't be hurt if it wasn't for me. You'd still be at Two and the other werewolves would still be together."

"Then Gem and the others in your father's center wouldn't have a chance of being rescued." Saying Gem's name sent a surge of frustration through me. I felt like I betrayed them both and couldn't make peace with the war in my heart.

"Jaze will get them out," she said. If she noticed the way my voice tightened when I said Gem's name, she didn't mention it. She waited a moment, then said softly, "I can't live without you, Vance. Life is empty when you're not there."

A warm tingle ran through my skin. I smoothed a finger along the calluses of my hand, noting the ridges formed by the silver bars of Lobotraz. "I'm not the same person I was."

"Neither of us is." Her voice was touched with sad bitterness and for the first time I realized what seeing her father in his true light had done to her.

I crossed the space between us and set a hesitant hand on her arm. She covered my fingers with her own. "You didn't have to leave your father for me."

"He's no longer my father," she replied, her beautiful green eyes full of pain at the statement. "Anyone who could do that to another person is no longer human."

"I'm not human," I pointed out gently.

She met my eyes. "You are to me."

My breath caught in my throat and I could barely breathe. I closed my eyes and felt her soft fingers caress the skin of my cheek. She touched me as though she knew all of my faults and weaknesses, and loved me for them. Strength and leadership had been the two traits my parents focused on at Two, the only things they seemed to care about. Weakness was attacked at Two until it was gone. The fact that she brought me to my knees with a simple glance should have brought her scorn, not her love. I didn't feel deserving of her trust and affection with the war that raged in my heart.

"Why me?" I breathed.

"You're the one that saved me, remember?" she replied with a hint of laughter in her voice. "Now you're stuck with me."

Want and need surged through me so strong I lowered my lips to hers and kissed her gently. I then brushed her cheek softly with my lips and whispered, "You are everything I hoped you would be and more." I swallowed and said, "I would choose to be stuck with you any day."

She smiled a beautiful, sweet smile and watched me walk away.

I waited until several turns of the rock walls were behind me, then pulled off my clothes and waited for the moonlight to take hold. I wanted more than anything to stay and just be in the moment with Nora, to forget Lobotraz, my torn emotions about Gem, the betrayal at Two, and the werewolves waiting in pain and discomfort for someone to free them. They, too, were phasing in the night and would have to face whatever torments Rob came up with until they were able to phase back to their human forms. The fact that tonight's phase would have meant my death by Rob's hands wasn't lost on me.

I took a deep breath and stepped into a circle of light on the path. The touch of moonlight wasn't necessary for the phase, but it felt right, more peaceful, to phase to wolf form under the gaze of the reverent moon. I glanced up and met Nora's eyes before the moon took hold. She watched me in silence as black fur grew over my body. The charred scars on my chest and back turned to white fur, making a strange pattern of light amid the black. I wanted to turn away, ashamed for some reason I couldn't explain as I phased, but her eyes held mine, nonjudgmental and loving without a trace of fear or loathing.

When I was done, Nora walked to me and knelt in the soft red sand. She put her arms around my neck and buried her face in my thick fur. She closed her eyes and breathed softly of the wolf scent that was mine. "I love you," she whispered.

I could only listen to her heartbeat and the soft brush of her breath against my fur. She kissed me gently on the forehead, then rose. "Go run; I'll be here when you get back."

A swell of gratitude rose in my chest. I trotted slowly down the trail and turned once to find her watching after me, a slight smile on her lips and a look of happiness in her spring green eyes. I hesitated, then went back to her and took her sleeve gently in my teeth. She followed me over the rise and I took her on a midnight tour of my favorite places in the desert.

\*\*\*

We pulled back into the garage at Jaze's safe house and found Jaze and Jet waiting for us. Jaze opened the door for Nora and waited until we were inside the house to speak. I appreciated the fact that he didn't ask where we had been. The scent of ash and desert sand that lingered on both of our skin probably brought questions to his mind, but he didn't push into matters that didn't involve him.

I was beginning to see how Jaze garnered the respect I saw on everyone's faces when they looked at him. It was as though he had the ability to take a person's strength and hone it so that they were appreciated for what they brought to the table. I didn't feel intimidated by the Alpha, rather accepted for my size and strength and allowed to make my own decisions.

"The Hunters and werewolves are assembled and awaiting my orders to join us at Lobotraz." He motioned for us to sit on a couch and sat in an armchair across from us. Jet stood by the open doorway, his muscles tense. His hands closed into fists and then opened again as though in anticipation of the coming fight, and his dark blue eyes glinted with thoughts he didn't voice.

"Hunters are fighting with us?" I asked, turning my attention back to Jaze.

He nodded. "Rob and the Hunters at Lobotraz are part of what we call the extremists. They refuse to comply with the peace agreements between Hunters and werewolves, and continue their hunting and killing. The Hunters that will fight with us have been there for me many times and I can trust them. They will provide the backup we need to storm Lobotraz."

Reluctance filling me at trusting a league of humans who had, as far as I knew, lived their whole lives with the motive of killing werewolves, but I knew we needed to get back to Lobotraz as soon as possible to save the other werewolves. I took a steeling breath. "Okay, where do we start?"

A scrawny werewolf with thin brown hair came into the room with a poster tube. The werewolf threw us a shy smile, then dropped his eyes and waited for Jaze to take the tube. Jaze dumped out the contents and unrolled a blueprint.

"This is Lobotraz."

I stared at it, amazed. "Where did you get that?"

Jaze smiled. "Let's just say Mouse has some, well, very particular skills that come in handy in times like these."

The thin werewolf smiled again and his cheeks turned red, but he refused to look at us.

Jaze motioned to the chart. "As you can see, Lobotraz is shaped like a wheel with spokes, the torture chambers and Rob's personal offices being at the center of that wheel and the various werewolf holding chambers branching out from it." He glanced at me. "We'll start at the opposite spoke from yours and work our way around in case yours is being monitored now."

"How do we get in?" I studied the blueprint intently, but the lines and panels made no sense to me besides the obvious corridors.

Jaze pointed to a small column running parallel to the spokes. "Here. The venting system runs along the top of each branch. We'll use them to get around and move as quietly as possible until we're caught."

"And then?" Nora asked.

Jaze smiled. "Then we show them what werewolves can really do."

Relief swelled my chest at finally being able to do something to stop Rob and free the werewolves under his guard. I nodded. "That sounds good to me."

Jaze rose and we followed. "My girlfriend, Nikki, has

breakfast ready in the kitchen if Jet's left us anything. We'll leave in a half hour."

# Chapter 16

Nora and I followed him to the kitchen where a girl I was surprised to smell was human had a dish of omelets and another of hash browns. The werewolf with the red eyes, Kaynan, joined us, followed by the one named Mouse. I stopped at the smell and my stomach turned over at the sight of something other than gray gruel in a silver bowl. Nora's fingers brushed my arm. "Are you alright?" she asked quietly.

Jaze turned back, the same question in his eyes.

I swallowed and nodded. "I can't- I can't remember the last time I had an omelet."

Nikki brushed her long black hair behind her shoulder with a quick flick of her wrist and handed me a plate. "Dive in. They're still warm and I've been fighting to keep them from Jet all morning."

I glanced up and saw Jet standing next to the back door, his eyes on the unfenced yard beyond. A smile might have touched his lips, but it vanished before I was sure. I accepted the plate and sat down at the table. Nora took the seat next to me and dished us both up. I had eyes only for the long yellow egg loafs stuffed with ham, cheese, peppers, tomatoes, onions, and bits of bacon. I had to fight down the urge to shove the whole thing in my mouth and cut a corner off with my fork, then lifted it to my tongue.

Flavors I had never before appreciated filled my mouth. The cheese was seasoned with a touch of pepper and just enough salt to accentuate the flavor of the eggs. The bacon taste lingered on my tongue with the promise of more to come, and the mild bite of the onions and peppers combated with the mild eggs. For half a second, I thought I would break down and cry in front of the werewolves and humans around me. I blinked quickly, determined not to let them think of me as a baby.

No one could understand how good something so simple could taste after three weeks of barely cooked leftovers from the slaughterhouse. I glanced up and saw a look of understanding sweep over Jet's face. He looked younger than me by about two years, but the memories of hunger and need that I saw in his eyes let me know that he had suffered far worse, and for a much longer time. His gaze met mine with the penetrating look of someone who has survived something so awful the memory lived just below the surface. He tipped his chin at my plate and indicated without saying anything that I should eat as much as I wanted without the worry of going hungry again.

I stared at him, amazed that someone could express so much without saying anything. He turned his face back toward the yard, but shadows swept through his dark blue eyes, etching his jaw as tight as granite as he looked through the memory to the sunlight that made shadows of the leaves on the grass. I took a calming breath and turned back to cut another corner off the omelet only to find two more crowding it on the plate.

"You looked hungry," Nikki said when I glanced up. The human girl smiled at me, completely comfortable in a room full of werewolves. She was about to dish another omelet onto Jaze's plate, but he declined and tipped his head toward me in a wolf-like gesture. Nikki smiled and scooped that omelet onto my plate as well. "It only makes sense that the biggest werewolf I've ever seen would have the biggest appetite," she commented before she went back to the stove.

I fought back a chuckle that might have turned into a sob and dove into the food, suddenly completely at ease despite the fact that I was surrounded by almost total strangers. Something in the air calmed me and I realized after a moment that it was Jaze. He conversed quietly with Kaynan, and the red-eyed werewolf watched him with the look of one who accepts the leadership of another even though they were equals.

The scent I got from Kaynan was strange. He smelled like a werewolf, but there was something chemical to the scent, like the tang of werewolf had been overlaid with something else that smelled almost human. He had black hair that showed a sheen of red when it caught the light, and some of his gestures, like the way he moved without much care and the way he ate appeared more human than werewolf. Werewolves savored the smell of food as much as the taste, but he ate his omelet as though he barely tasted it. Maybe he was just hungry.

I finished the omelets and several helpings of hash browns while I watched Jaze with his team. Mouse brought a computer in and ran something by him. Jaze agreed and Mouse disappeared back into another room without making eye contact with me. I had seen other grays that were submissive, but the way he took every word from Jaze without question kept my attention. Either they had worked together for a long enough time that they trusted each others' every move, or Jaze had more control over his team than I imagined.

"How are you holding up?" Nikki asked.

I looked up to answer, then realized she was talking to Nora.

"Alright," Nora replied. She picked up my empty plate and hers and carried them to the sink. "You guys have been so kind."

"I know it hasn't been easy," Nikki said in a soft tone of understanding. She glanced back at Jaze; when her blue eyes met his, a warm smile passed between them. "But we're always glad to have the company, aren't we Jaze?"

He nodded. "Most definitely. You two are welcome to stay here as long as you'd like. We'll be returning home when things at Lobotraz are resolved, and my mother would love to have you over."

"The more the merrier," Nikki concluded, and the others laughed.

Jaze's phone rang and he answered it, then stood up. "Time to go. The choppers are waiting."

The thought that we would be taking helicopters surprised me, and I saw the same feeling cross Nora's face. Jaze apparently had much more pull than I imagined. I tried to convince Nora to stay behind, but she refused, saying that she wanted to make sure her father was brought to justice for the crimes he had committed. I worried how she would feel when her father was truly in custody of Jaze's team, but it was her father and I didn't feel I had the right to argue after what we both had gone through at his hand. I gave in, but regretted the decision when we reached the location of Lobotraz.

"It's a dam?" I asked, confused.

Jaze shook his head. "It's under the dam." At my look, he gestured to several small camouflaged lumps that looked like rocks on top of the small rise near the edge of the water. On further scrutiny, they turned out to be ventilation openings for a cooling system. "We'll start in the branch opposite from yours. I have four teams going down. They'll signal us if they run into trouble. We'll work both ways around until we run into opposition; our goal is to get every werewolf out of Lobotraz."

As much as I wanted to go straight to Gem and free her immediately, his logic made sense. "Fine, but I'm going in first."

He nodded as if he had expected as much and handed me something wrapped in a cloth. I took it and the rag fell away to reveal a small handgun. I glanced at Jaze.

His face was grim. "These men will kill any of us on sight.

Be prepared to at least wound them and take their weapons, but don't be a hero. The only way to save the werewolves down there and stop Rob and the extremists is to hit hard and fast. They probably know we're coming and they'll be instructed to bring you down, so remember the lack of mercy they show and repay it in kind."

My chest tightened at the thought of killing again, but the memory of the pain I had faced at their hands surged through my scars as though to remind me of the cruelty below. I checked the safety and made sure there was a bullet in the chamber, then nodded. "Right. Let's go."

Twenty SUVs had been parked about a mile back, and almost a hundred Hunters and werewolves waited for Jaze's orders. They were a quiet, orderly lot, and respect and pride showed in their faces when they looked at Jaze. There was definitely more to the werewolf than I knew from our brief encounters, and I hoped there would be time later to get to know the one who got me out of Lobotraz. The thought of entering it again after all that had happened turned my stomach cold, but I forced my expression to remain calm and confident.

Two Hunters pried up one of the rock structures to reveal a pipe below. Other teams worked on the other ventilation shafts, and soon four of the structures around the dam had been moved to reveal rectangular steel piping. I glanced back at Jaze. "You sure they don't have these guarded after you guys broke me out?"

Jaze shook his head. "Not positive, but we covered our tracks well. I'm hoping it looked like you vanished into thin air."

The thought made me smile. "That would give Rob something to think about." I took a deep breath and lowered myself down the pipe. My werewolf eyesight made flashlights unnecessary, though the Hunters that would come down last carried them. Nora dropped down next to me and took a firm grip on my hand. "It's going to be alright," I whispered to her.

"I know," she replied. "I just can't wait to get the others out."

I moved slowly forward, my soft-soled shoes quiet against the cold metal. Soft thuds announced more werewolves climbing down the pipe. Jaze would be after Nora, with Jet and Kaynan following. A group of hand-picked Hunters whom Jaze reassured me he had worked with on countless rescues would bring up the rear. The thought of Jaze's team covering Nora's back was reassuring.

A thousand possibilities of what could go wrong flashed through my mind. If they were waiting for us, the pipes were sealed, Rob wasn't at Lobotraz, or if the werewolves had been moved to a new location altogether taunted my thoughts. I shoved them away and followed the pipe on a steep decline below the water of the dam. Claustrophobia rose at the thought of being beneath so much water. If I had known where Lobotraz was before, it would have been that much harder to stay in the cage.

The smell twisted my stomach with recognition. Unwashed bodies, festering wounds, fear, refuse, hopelessness, and rotten food drifted through the pipe to announce that we were close. I gritted my teeth and stopped at the first mesh opening.

"Hold," Jaze whispered from just behind Nora. He listened to something in his ear piece, then motioned for me to move forward. "Cameras are cut," he said. "We'll have to move quickly."

I pulled the screen back and dropped to the floor of the narrow room. The inhabitants looked only slightly interested and I remembered my own reaction when Jaze and Jet came to my cell. It felt like a mirage brought by pain, and then just another of Rob's cruel torments. I ached for them because I knew too well what they were going through.

I reached up and helped Nora to the ground, then Jaze, Jet, Kaynan, and four other werewolves jumped down to join us. Whispers of fabric and light footsteps heralded werewolves and Hunters moving to the next rooms from the vents above.

"We're here to get you out," I said softly. I knew they wouldn't believe me, but it felt better than saying nothing.

A werewolf stepped forward with a bolt cutter and began to cut his way down the row. The gun felt cold in my hand. I shoved it behind my belt and opened the first cage. The bite of the silver was harsher having been away from it, and I regretted not bringing gloves. The werewolf inside stared at me with baleful, hazy eyes. I stepped toward him and he cringed against the back of the cage.

"No, don't," I said quietly. His bare back touched the bars, but he was numb to the pain. A tremor ran through my limbs in response as I bent and gathered his frail body in my arms. He didn't protest when I carried him from the cage and handed him to one of the werewolves under the vent.

I watched as he was lifted up to the pipe and pulled carefully inside. The werewolves and Hunters that lined the ventilation shaft up to the mouth would help him climb the steep rise; others beyond were set to rush each werewolf to a waiting vehicle.

Jaze and Jet were already inside the next two cages. I hurried to the fourth where Nora stood staring at a form inside. I used the hem of my shirt to pull open the door, but I could tell by the odor of decay that the werewolf had died a few days ago. I covered the still form with the ratty blanket discarded in the opposite corner, which told me more about the occupant than I could put into words. I touched the body one more time, then closed the cage door behind me feeling as though I left a piece of my soul inside. One more night and I would have died like him.

"He's dead?" Nora whispered, horror tightening her voice.

I nodded, realized her vision was limited in the faint lighting, and forced my voice to remain calm despite the way my heart pounded in my ears. "Yes, but we need to worry about the other werewolves now, the ones we can save."

"My father will pay for this," she said, rage giving her voice strength.

"That's why we're here," I reminded her gently.

I pulled open the door to the next cage, then bit back a growl when I saw the condition of the occupant. She was curled in the corner, the scraps of her blanket inadequately covering her lashed body. Black whip burns covered her skin from head to toe and my own scars gave a sympathetic throb.

I pulled off my shirt and wrapped it around her. She lifted her head weakly and gave me a small smile. "I knew you'd come back," Gem's voice drifted from the battered body. I blinked and recognized the pixie cut blond hair and blue eyes despite her bruised, swollen face.

"What did they do to you?" I demanded.

She shrugged, then winced and seemed to curl in on herself to stop the pain. "They wanted to know where you went."

"That's ridiculous. You weren't even there when I escaped." An inferno of rage flowed through my body so swiftly my hands shook and I had to take several breaths to keep from phasing.

"Apparently one of the other werewolves told them we talked sometimes." Anger must have flashed through my eyes because she set a frail hand on my arm. "They said it to save their skin, and it wasn't a lie. They didn't know this would happen." She took a shallow breath as though her ribs hurt.

"When they couldn't find out anything, they separated us so we wouldn't help each other. If anyone talked, they came in and beat us again."

"I'm getting you out of here," I said. I picked her up as gently as I could, but I heard her breath catch at the pain of each movement. Her head lolled against my shoulder. "I'm so sorry," I whispered.

"I told you I'd be rescued," she replied with a shadow of a smile that hinted at her former self.

"You were right," I agreed. My heart ached at her pain and soared to be near her again. I wanted to protect her from everything bad that had happened, to get her far away from Lobotraz and help her escape the haunting nightmares that would follow as they did for me. I had to remind myself that other werewolves needed me. As much as I wanted to take care of Gem, our rescue was bigger than just the two of us. I carried her gently down the aisle between the cages.

Jet waited under the vent. I was reluctant to let Gem go, but the chance of seeking revenge against Rob was too great to turn away now. I passed Gem to the black-haired werewolf. "Take care of her," I said.

Understanding showed in Jet's dark eyes so stark and painful it was as though he knew exactly what we had gone through. "She'll be safe with me," he said in a voice full of black emotion that echoed the tormented places in my heart.

I watched her disappear into the pipe above, took a calming breath to collect myself, then hurried with Nora to the other end of the room.

"Is she a friend?" she asked in a whisper.

"She was in the cage next to mine," I replied. A memory of her handing over a cup of water to wash the silver from my feet flashed into my mind and I blinked back tears. "She was beaten because of me."

"She was beaten because of my dad," Nora replied. "You

can't help that you were a prisoner here. It's my fault they caught you."

I shook my head, but didn't reply. Gem was all I could think about. Her beaten body and the look of suffering in her eyes stilled my heart. She had gone through all of that because of me. My heart clenched at the thought of her in pain and I couldn't forgive myself for how long she had waited for us to come back. She hadn't given up.

Gem was so strong in ways that dwarfed anyone else I had met. The fact that she was still alive brought tears to my eyes. I vowed to see her pain-free and healthy again, full of food that would help put weight back on her skinny frame, basking in light and sunshine, and under starlight and the reassuring presence of the moon. I would take care of her. I gritted my teeth and turned back to the job at hand. Nora hesitated, then hurried after me.

Jet and Jaze were lifting the final werewolf to the Hunters above when someone pounded on the door at the end of the room. Jet had slipped a chain through the handles and secured it with a snap hook. The last werewolf cleared the vent opening and Kaynan and two Hunters jumped down to join us as the vent was closed tightly from above.

Jaze pulled a gun from behind his belt. He flashed me a serious look. "Ready?"

I pulled the gun from my belt as well and slid off the safety. "Ready."

Jet and Kaynan waited on each side of the door. Nora kept back with the Hunters past the last row of cages to be out of the heart of battle. Jaze and I reached the door on silent feet. The banging had stopped, but shadows blocked out the light from the hallway beyond and angry voices came through.

Jet silently unfastened the snap hook and lifted the chain out of the door handles, careful to not make a noise. He coiled it around his right hand. He didn't carry a gun, but he pulled a knife that looked just as deadly from a sheath around his ankle.

Kaynan made similar preparations on the other side, except the knife he used came from a wristband on his arm. I didn't see how he pulled it out, but he unfastened the band and then a blade glinted in the darkness. He and Jet exchanged a charged glance. Both looked ready for whatever would come through that door. I wondered what kind of a lifestyle involved an expectation toward killing.

# Chapter 17

Jet looped two fingers loosely around the door handle and waited for Jaze's signal. Jaze listened to his headpiece, then nodded. My heart thundered in my chest. I wondered if I would recognize the guards, if they would be the pair that jostled prisoners the least, or the four who made every day a living nightmare. Maybe Rob had replaced all of his guards after my disappearance. I didn't have to imagine what he would do to anyone who got on his bad side.

Jet pulled open the door and Jaze shot the first two forms that appeared. I didn't have time to see their faces against the silhouette of the neon lighting in the hallway before they slumped to either side. Jaze glanced back just as someone else forced his way through. A gunshot sounded next to me and the body collapsed. I looked back to find Nora with a gun raised, the acrid scent of smoke wafting from the end. At my shocked look, her cheeks touched red and she dropped her eyes. "Somebody had to do it."

"Thanks," Jaze replied. He took a steeling breath, then pushed through the door with Jet at his side. Kaynan and I followed them at a swift trot down the hall to a set of double doors at the end. The Hunters and Nora went slower to intercept anyone who came up behind us. Before we could reach the doors, shots rang out.

I spun and dropped to one knee, taking aim like I had done a million times at Two during practice. The forty-five in my hand weighed more than the one I was used to, but it responded to the slightest squeeze of the trigger. A succession of bullets rang out from our side, bringing down the six guards who appeared at the corner.

I let out a breath, then a dozen more guards appeared. I ran toward Nora and pulled her into my arms, shielding her with my body as Jaze's team took out our attackers. Nora trembled in my arms, but as soon as the firing stopped, she lifted her gun, ready to defend us both.

Ballistic shields appeared next carried by six heavily armed men. They ducked behind the thick metal as our bullets ricocheted off. Submachine guns appeared at the top of the shields. I knew the second they pulled their triggers, the entire team would be wiped out. Jaze's werewolves were behind me, and the Hunters huddled around us. There wasn't time for anyone to take action.

I pushed Nora to the ground out of harm's way and took two running steps. I leaped over the shields and phased in the air before I hit the ground. The guns followed my path as the guards turned to defend themselves, leaving their backs unprotected for a brief moment.

It was the split second we needed. Two black blurs and one red one jumped over the forgotten shields and tore into our attackers. Growls and yells rang out, turning the hallway into a cacophony of pain-filled screams as we took down the threat. Within minutes, only a mass of bodies lay at our feet.

Blood colored my muzzle when I looked up at Nora and the Hunters watching from the middle of the hallway. There was no disgust on Nora's face, only fear that I hoped came from being under fire by the guards. I stepped around the corner and phased, then pulled on what was left of my tattered clothes. Jaze, Jet, and Kaynan followed a few seconds later, their muzzles as red as mine had been.

Kaynan's crimson fur made him look like a creature out of a horror story. I wondered what had happened to make him so different from other werewolves. The two black wolves beside him phased quickly and I found Jet watching me. "That was brave," he said quietly.

"A bit foolhardy," Kaynan replied with a teasing light in his red eyes.

I smiled. "It was the first thing I could think of."

Jaze handed me my gun. "We owe you for that."

I tipped my head to indicate Lobotraz in general. "Consider us even."

He nodded seriously and they followed me back up the hall to where Nora and the Hunters waited. Nora checked me over quickly like she expected to see bullet holes dotting my body, and finding none, she threw her arms around my neck. "You need to be more careful," she said in a chiding tone that almost covered the underlying quaver.

"I'll try," I promised her. I glanced at Jaze. "Let's finish this."

He nodded and motioned to the double doors at the end. He and Jet each took a door, then he checked his watch. I wondered what they were waiting for. Anxiety filled my chest at what we would find beyond. The noise in the hall should have alerted anyone who waited in the central room. The element of surprise was no longer on our side. Given Jaze's attack plan, no one could have escaped down the branching hallways from the center. If Rob was there, we would have to use brute force to bring him down.

A few seconds later, the lights went out, flooding the entire compound in darkness. Jaze and Jet pushed through the doors. I let Kaynan and one of the Hunters go by, then fell in beside Nora. She threw me a grateful look, her figure menacing with a gun held in her hands like she knew how to use it. After seeing her shoot, I didn't doubt her abilities. She pushed strands of hair off her face and her brow creased with determination. My heart thrummed at a steady, low pace, my phasing instincts under control as long as we had the upper hand.

We followed Jaze's team into the main center of Lobotraz. Computers glared in stark contrast to the darkness around us while a generator hummed noisily in a corner. A strange, sharp odor colored the air, masking the scent of anyone who might be hiding in the room.

"Stay back," Jaze warned softly. He and Jet began to sweep the left side of the low-ceilinged area while Kaynan and the Hunters took the right. Both teams walked silently through the room like lethal shadows, their footsteps barely audible on the cement floor.

Figures appeared near the front of the room and shots rang out. The teams dove behind desks and returned fire. I pulled Nora away from the doorway and we ducked down behind a set of filing cabinets. Nora scooted to the far end. I followed her, checking over my shoulder to make sure more guards didn't appear at the door.

A hand shot out and wrapped around Nora's neck. A gun was pressed tightly to her head. My breath caught in my throat when Rob appeared triumphantly behind her. The sight of his face sent a surge of rage so strong through my body that all I could think of was ending his life to stop the torture. I aimed my gun at the bit of his face that I could see. I took a steady breath, then blinked and saw Nora's wide eyes just to the right of my target. Her face grew pale with terror as the gun pressed harder into her temple. I lowered my weapon.

"Well, well, if it isn't the vanishing werewolf," Rob said. His hand tightened around Nora's neck. "Along with my errant daughter."

"Let her go, Rob," I growled. My heart pounded in my chest. The gun shook in my grip and I couldn't trust my aim.

"After I just found her again?" he replied. He backed up, dragging her with him.

Nora's eyes held mine, begging me to free her. I looked around, but couldn't see a way to flank him in the tight quarters between the desks. Both sets of werewolves were being held back by shots fired from the far end of the room. Rob pulled Nora back with him toward his guards. A dark mahogany desk took up the entire length of one wall with filing cabinets on either side. The guards ducked behind it when Jaze's team returned fire.

"You don't deserve her," I growled.

Rob's eyebrows lifted and a mocking smile showed at the corners of his mouth. "And you do?" He pulled her around the dark desk. I took a step to follow them, but he motioned me away with the gun. Several bullets whizzed past and I ducked back behind the filing cabinet. "Stay over there, and she won't get hurt," Rob said. The honesty of his words sent a chill through my body. He would hurt her to get to me. I couldn't risk her life, but I also couldn't sit by and do nothing.

I flanked him on the outside of the table. Jaze and Kaynan fired at the guards to keep them out of sight; the bullets that flew by me barely registered in the face of Nora in danger. For the briefest instant, I entertained the thought of jumping over the desk and crushing Rob with the weight of my body, drawing his fire to me instead of Nora. I crouched to spring just as Rob reached under the desk.

A loud explosion sounded. I was thrown backward as debris and wood flew around the room. A deep, shuddering noise reverberated above me. I glanced up to see massive cracks run through the ceiling, thick fissures parting the cement. Another shudder sounded, then the roof caved in. A chunk of cement bigger than one of the desks crashed on top of me and pinned me to the ground. Nora screamed my name, but her voice was faint as though she was no longer in the room. Water began to flow around my body as I struggled to get free. Blood streamed through my hair from the explosion. I tried to push up, but the cement was too heavy.

"Quick, get it off him," Jaze shouted.

The pressure of the cement eased slightly. A pair of hands grabbed my ankles and tried to pull me free, but my shoulders were trapped. Water rushed up past my face. I struggled against the hands and the cement, heedless of the way the rocks tore my skin. My breath screamed in my chest. The cement shifted again. Several hands grabbed my arms. I put all my strength into one last surge and pushed out. The cement tipped to the side and hands slid me free.

I sat up gasping for air. Water poured from the huge gap in the ceiling and it was obvious that if we didn't move quickly, we would all drown.

Hands held pressure to the back of my head. "Can you stand?" Jaze asked above the roar of water filling the room. "Rob and Nora disappeared during the collapse. We have to find them." He put a hand to his ear to muffle the roar of water. "Tris, Roger, there's a breach in the dam. Get everyone out now!"

I stood up gingerly. Red touched the corners of my vision and a black wave danced in front of my eyes. I stumbled forward, but Jaze and Kaynan caught me. Jaze's concerned eyes met mine. "Rob and Nora disappeared behind this wall. There's a catch somewhere and we have to find it before the room fills. You know Nora's scent best; we'll search with you." .

I took a steeling breath and straightened up. I touched the back of my head and my fingers came away bloody. I gritted my teeth and made my way around the debris-covered desk. Water reached half-way up the mahogany now. If it wasn't for the others, I would have drowned under the cement. I shuddered and pressed forward, but the only thing on the other side of the desk was a flat gray wall.

I ran my hands along the cement. The cool, moistened rock refused to reveal its secrets. I tried to calm the chaos swirling through my mind. It took all of my concentration to push away the thunder of water pouring from the hole and Jaze's shouted commands as he directed his men. I closed my eyes and pictured Nora, her green eyes and her long black hair. I moved slowly back and forth in front of the wall, my eyes still closed and hands keeping me steady.

The pounding in my head increased with each step to the point that the pain clouded every other sense. I was about to give up when a faint breath touched my face. A teasing tendril of vanilla and sunflowers tangled within it. I dropped to my knees and dug at the bricks.

"Did you find something?" Jaze asked, kneeling beside me.

"Fresh air," I replied. I pointed and searched the area around us for the trigger.

Jaze put his face to it. "You're right," he breathed. He stood up and began feeling around the desk for something we had missed.

I couldn't find a purchase in the stone. The water level was up to our waists and Jaze's men were returning.

"Found it," Jaze called over his shoulder. He slid something under the water near the foot of the desk and the panel moved in front of me to reveal a winding staircase.

"Lead them up," I said to Kaynan; there was no time to question protocol about giving orders to someone else's pack mate.

Kaynan didn't question and ran up the stairs. Jet and two other werewolves followed close behind.

I turned and met Jaze's gaze.

"You first," he said.

"What about you?" I asked.

"I have to make sure my team gets out," Jaze replied.

"I'm not leaving until all the prisoners are gone."

He nodded, a gleam of respect in his eyes. "My thoughts exactly."

Werewolves, Hunters, and Rob's men who were now our prisoners pushed quickly up the stairs. Jaze's team called to each other, keeping up contact as they helped the others out of the flooding room. The water was nearly to the roof and we had to swim to keep our heads above it by the time the guards gave word that the last werewolf was through. Jaze checked his earpiece one last time, then motioned me in.

"You first," I said.

He looked like he wanted to argue, then he ducked through the door and left me in the control room. Objects floated menacingly in the dark water, my imagination giving reaching hands to dark chairs and office equipment. One of Rob's cat-o-nine-tails lay tangled on an empty file box that floated above his desk. My stomach twisted and I ducked through the opening to the staircase.

The stairs turned into an upward-sloping ramp that ended about a half-mile from Lobotraz. The pounding from the back of my head increased until I had to lean against the wall to walk. Jaze met me half-way up and threw one of my arms over his shoulders. "Thought you decided to stay behind."

"Just wanted to make sure no one else would suffer in there," I replied. I glanced at him. "Any sign of Nora?"

Jaze's eyes darkened. "They were gone before Kaynan and the others reached the surface. There's no sign of where they went. I have my team searching for trails."

I cursed softly and hit the wall. I was a fool; I shouldn't have let her come along. Her life was in her father's hands again, and I didn't doubt he would keep her under lock and key this time, if not worse.

"Hang in there," Jaze said quietly, an edge of command to his voice. "Don't give up on us. We got your werewolves out, didn't we?" I glanced at him. He met my gaze steadily. "I don't stop until everyone is safe."

His words reminded me of my own determination to take care of the werewolves at Two. "That can be a challenging task."

He gave a small smile and helped me step forward. "Tell me about it."

We walked slowly up the ramp and I leaned more heavily on him than I liked. He didn't seem bothered by my weight, and I wondered how strong the werewolf really was. My head pounded with each step. Jaze's werewolves and Hunters waited for us at the exit to Lobotraz. Jaze refused to step aside and let someone else help me. He walked at my side to the vehicles and made sure I was sitting comfortably before he turned away to give orders to those who waited for him. My respect for the werewolf grew with every action I observed. Jaze was truly someone worthy of the respect he quietly commanded.

I leaned against the SUV, letting the pain of my aching head dull the agony of losing Nora. I had failed her, and for all I knew she was going to a situation worse than mine had been at Lobotraz. I buried my head in my hands, so angry at myself and the world I wished I would have jumped in front of Rob's gun and saved Nora.

"Are you alright?" I looked up to see a brown-haired werewolf with blue-gray eyes watching me. She held bandages in one hand and indicated my head. "That needs to be wrapped."

I crouched down against the vehicle so she could reach my head and her nimble fingers swiftly tied bandages securely against the damaged flesh. When she finished, she stepped back and looked me over. "I think you'll live," she said with a smile. "I've seen worse."

Jet helped an injured werewolf walk past and her eyes lit up at seeing him. "Jet!" He helped the werewolf into an SUV, then came back over and gave her a quick kiss, his dark eyes and expression lightening just from being near her. "Another arena down, Taye," he said in a reference I didn't understand.

"They're getting worse," Taye replied with concern in her

eyes.

He nodded and she slipped her hand into his.

I leaned against Mouse's SUV and watched bony, bruised, worn werewolves climb into the vehicles around us. Hope shone on some of their faces, but others barely showed a flicker of emotion at the change in surroundings.

"Vance!" a voice called. My heart soared, chasing all other thoughts from my mind. I turned just before Gem slammed into me, her petite arms wrapping tightly around my neck and her blue eyes bright; the fresh wounds along her body had to hurt, but she didn't show it. "I told you we'd get out! I just didn't know you'd be the one to do it!"

I lowered her gingerly back to the sand, her skinny frame sharp under my hands. "I didn't know, either." It felt so good to be near her again, like an empty part of my heart filled to overflowing in her presence. Seeing her in the sunlight drove the thought home that I could truly be happy with her. She was a werewolf and we had been through so much together. But part of my heart longed after Nora, after her calming touch and the way she knew everything about me and accepted me for who I was. Gem smiled up at me and I couldn't hide the torment that swept through my mind.

"Are you alright?" she asked, her voice touched with concern.

I pushed away the troubling thoughts. "After all you've been through, you ask if I'm okay?" I leaned down swiftly and without thinking, kissed her lightly on the lips.

She laughed and hugged me harder than I thought her frail body could manage. I glanced up and found Jaze watching us, a light of understanding in his eyes. I ducked my head to hide the war within. It felt right to kiss Gem, but something was missing. I took a breath and tried to clear the chaos of emotions that swirled through my mind.

Gem tipped her head back at the others. "What are we

going to do with them?"

"Rehabilitation," Jaze answered. He stood a few feet away overseeing the werewolves as they were assisted into the waiting vehicles. "Then we'll find their homes." His brow creased. "Most of my rehab centers are full. We'll have to split everyone up."

I shook my head and ran a finger across my knuckles. "It'd be nice to keep them all together. I think it'll help the recovery process." A thought occurred to me and the rightness of it surged through my body. "I have the resources. Let me build them a place."

Jaze's eyebrows lifted. "Are you sure?"

I nodded. "I need something to do." I didn't say that I would go crazy until we found Nora, but I could tell Jaze understood.

He nodded. "Thank you."

# Chapter 18

"I'm just so glad you're alive," Mom's voice crackled on the other end of the phone. I forced down a surge of emotion at her voice. "I can't tell you how worried I've been. You don't return any of my emails."

After Lobotraz, I couldn't bring myself to call home. The complete abandonment I experienced there made it that much harder to dial Mom's number and hear it confirmed. I emailed her at Gem's insistence using one of Mouse's computers and briefly detailed my escape, Jaze's help, and Nora's disappearance, and asked for the funding we needed to build a rehabilitation center. I couldn't bring myself to open any of the numerous emails she sent in reply.

Gem finally convinced me that it was sheer stubbornness that kept me from calling her. She borrowed a phone and made me promise to call because as she put it, it was the most important thing I could do at the time. I accepted the phone reluctantly, but couldn't resist the pleading in Gem's bright blue eyes. It was enough to see her eating and growing healthier each day. After all she had been through, I couldn't refuse her anything. I finally promised and watched her skip around in glee with a cheerful smile on her face.

Now I stood on a red rock outcropping overseeing the building of the rehab center in an effort to keep my mind busy. A square of glass carried by one of the werewolves caught the light of the sun and bounced it toward me. I closed my eyes. "Any luck finding Nora?" I asked, though I knew if she heard anything she would have called me immediately.

"No." Her answer came reluctantly. "But we're sweeping everywhere. I can't imagine a flea could get through."

"Yet she has," I whispered too quietly for her to hear. I cleared my throat. "Thanks, Mom. Keep me posted."

"I will," she promised. She hesitated. "Vance?" My heart closed away from the emotion in her voice. "We're so glad you're alright."

"I'm not alright, Mother," I admitted. "But finding Nora will help with that a great deal.

"We'll find her," she vowed.

"Talk to you later." I hung up the phone and studied the landscape. The azure sky hung above the red sandstone like a jewel. A knot formed in my throat at the thought of telling Nora about the same sky and the way it held me at Two. The color reminded me of Nora so starkly I could barely breathe.

The location was perfect for the new rehabilitation center. It was situated far enough from Two that Rob couldn't find us if Nora broke down and told him where we were, but it was still in the red rock desert that my soul called home. Mom was as good as her word and building crews had arrived at the land the moment she purchased it. I was happy to see the money used for good, and felt grateful for the first time that my mother spared no expense when I asked for help.

Walls were being erected and Gem worked with several of the others who had enough strength to help out. They felt as I did. When they weren't busy, thoughts of Lobotraz and the nightmares within its walls barraged down like the water of the dam. Though Jet's girlfriend Taye was on hand to make sure they took breaks when needed, the werewolves were happy to help build something out of the wreckage that had become their lives.

Mouse, the small, skinny werewolf that had a knack for electronics, fiddled in a main room that was already stocked with computers despite the lack of walls. He was obviously anxious to be back in touch with Jaze's command center despite our remote location. Gem skipped into the room, handed the werewolf something small and metal that gleamed in the light, then smiled when he blushed as he said thank you. She skipped back out of the room and I wondered if Mouse felt as I did, that it was lighter for her having been in it.

I watched Gem move within the construction zone. She wore a yellow hardhat on her head that slid from side to side as she bounced over beams of wood and building debris like a woodland fairy. She had dyed her blond pixie cut hair pink, and Nikki, Jaze's human girlfriend, had helped her trim the ends so it fit her sprightly personality. I had never seen someone with so much energy. It was like now that she had escaped the confines of the bars, she couldn't be contained.

She glanced up, caught me watching her, and flashed a happy smile that touched her blue eyes and made her practically glow. I waved and a surge of longing welled up in my chest. But now that she was here, the need wasn't for the touch of her hand or to see her safe. I missed the scent of vanilla and sunflowers; I wanted the one who wasn't safely below working with werewolves to build strong walls and beautiful floors. I had serious issues.

I slid down the sides of two narrow canyon walls until my shoes hit the dirt with a red puff. I pushed through the narrow red rock tunnels and entered a small sand arena feeling like I was going to explode if I didn't hit something. I squared up with one of the walls and began to beat it with my bare knuckles, letting the bite of the rock chase the pain from my chest.

Rob's face loomed in my mind with his overly confident expression above his tailored suit. I punched the wall harder. The surface grew slick and the burning in my knuckles eased the ache in my heart at the thought of Nora in Rob's possession. My side began to throb. Nora's green eyes bright with concern the way she had looked when we climbed from the flash flood rose to my mind. The fact that she had been the one to send Jaze to Lobotraz and save me from that horrible prison sent guilt through my chest. I couldn't find her. After all we had gone through, I was the one letting her down.

I staggered forward and leaned against the wall. Tears stained my cheeks. I wiped them away with the back of my hand and felt more moisture. I glanced down and found that my knuckles were coated in blood from hitting the wall. The skin was peeled away and the stinging throb of sweat burned the edges. I dug the heels of my hands into my eyes to stop the futile tears. Tears were a coward's way out and wouldn't save her.

Unable to stand being under the azure sky without Nora any longer, I tore off my clothes, phased, and barreled through the narrow red rock passage. A form jumped out of my way. My nose identified Jaze's scent, but I couldn't think past the need for the dry, arid air of the desert and the harsh, unforgiving landscape. I lowered my head, pulled my ears back, and ran.

\*\*\*

I didn't realize until the smell of death and decay filled my nose that my paws had taken me to White Horse Canyon. The troubled air told of the bodies below before I even reached the rim. I skidded to a stop, my tongue out and chest heaving. The bodies in the canyon beyond had been Nora's friends. I had killed them all.

I glared into the depths below, hating myself for the pain I had caused them, for the mothers and fathers who had lost sons and daughters and would never know where they went, for the pain on Nora's face when I told her they were dead, and for the sightless eyes that had stared up at me accusingly that first night because I had lived when they died.

The heavy smell tangled through my fur, threatening to drag me down with them. I snorted and backed up. Red sand scuffed around my paws bruised from beating the wall. I lowered my head to the sand and tried to lose the smell of decay amid the cinnamon and sage scent of the dirt, but the stench refused to leave. I turned and ran from the canyon as fast as I could. I couldn't chase away the thought that I had been running from everything my whole life, everything but Nora.

I reached the end of the canyon when a shadow caught up to me and I barely avoided crashing into Jaze. He sidestepped easily and watched me as I regained my footing. I didn't know how long he had been following me. The fact that he was here, in my red rocks, bothered me but I couldn't say why. I owed Jaze my life. I think just being near Two and the places where I grew up rattled my thoughts.

I studied Jaze, a black wolf whose fur blended almost perfectly into the shadows. I blinked and realized that it was night. My run had taken me longer than I thought. Guilt at leaving the others working flooded me and I lowered my head. I trotted slowly to one of the clothes caches still hidden among the rocks and phased, then pulled on a pair of black shorts and a worn gray shirt. I tossed a second set of clothes to Jaze and he phased, then waited for me without speaking.

We walked silently along the soft sand that felt as fine as powder underfoot. I never wore shoes in the desert. They were too constricting and the feeling of sand between my toes was home as much as the rock walls around us. The scent of sage baked by the sun lingered beneath the starlit sky, and the stars that twinkled down glowed brightly through their midnight canvas.

"They're brighter out here," Jaze said quietly, breaking our silence.

I glanced at him. "What?"

He tipped his head to indicate the stars. "At home, I can barely see a dozen in the sky. Too much light from the city." He fell silent, then said, "It's better, being out here under the stars. It feels like we're all connected somehow."

I looked up at them again. To me they had always just been there, the constellations floating slowly across the dark expanse, phantoms of stories older than the world I knew. Walking beneath them again after the weeks spent in Lobotraz felt surreal. I couldn't decide which experience was more of a dream.

"I know you're worried about Nora," Jaze said when I didn't say anything. "I've got every werewolf and Hunter here and in the adjoining states on the lookout. When Rob surfaces, we'll know."

I took a breath of night air and let it flow out between my teeth. "I'm worried about her, but there's so much more to it."

"The werewolf, Gem," Jaze said.

I glanced at him in surprise, then remembered that he had seen our small kiss outside of Lobotraz. I nodded. "I don't know what's wrong with me. I feel so selfish." The words surprised me. I had never opened up to the other Alphas at Two. I was supposed to be the tough one, the one who had everything figured out even though we were all lost in our own ways. But it felt like once the gate was opened, the words wouldn't stay in. "Nora completes my heart in ways I could never imagine. She's smart, spunky, brave beyond doubt, and willing to stand up for what she believes in even against her father."

I paused and Jaze nodded. "She's a wonderful girl," he said quietly.

I agreed, but I shook my head. "But something happened at Lobotraz. I was at the point. . . ." It was hard to say what I needed to. I swallowed and continued, "At the point of giving up, but Gem pulled me through. I owe her my life, and she deserves to be happy."

"Do you love her?"

I stopped walking and stared at Jaze. "What?"

He faced me, his expression serious. "Do you love Gem?"

I was about to give a flippant answer, but I owed him more; by the expression on his face, I knew he expected more from me as well. I rubbed my eyes with one hand in an effort to clear my thoughts. "Yes, but in a different way from Nora."

He nodded as if he had guessed as much. "You said you feel complete with Nora. Do you feel the same way with Gem?"

I thought that I did. I pictured her hand in mine, the grime of Rob's catacombs around us. I saw her blue eyes shine so brightly under the sun. I felt my lips on her for the brief second next to the car. I wanted to nod, to accept that she was what I wanted, that I should be with a werewolf instead of a human, but I owed it to both of us to be honest.

I shook my head.

"You know werewolves mate for life," Jaze said. "And we don't necessarily choose our mate; when she steps into your life, it feels like she was chosen before you ever met."

I nodded. I had felt the exact same when I saw Nora for the first time fighting for her life against the werewolves of Two. When her eyes met mine, something drove home so powerfully I protected her against every instinct in my body. "But she's human," I said.

A touch of humor lit Jaze's eyes. "It doesn't have to make sense."

"But it should," I replied before I could stop myself. In all of my studies, races survived on natural selection and survival of the fittest. My mother would scream if she knew how much I truly loved Nora. I came from a long line of werewolves with pure wolven blood. No human had ever tainted the family line. Shame filled me that I thought of it as such. Maybe I was just as blind as my parents.

"You've met Nikki, right?" Jaze asked; his eyes narrowed slightly with his smile. I nodded, but when I didn't say anything, he let out a breath. "I fell for her hard, harder than I wanted to admit. And believe me, it was not a pleasant time for a werewolf to be in love with a Hunter."

I watched him carefully, the way his eyes lit up when he talked of his girlfriend, the crease in his forehead when he told about the Hunters and the way they used to be. Sorrow shone in his gaze when he spoke of finding his father dead, killed by Hunters and his uncle in an attempt to wipe out the Alphas. "Uniting Hunters and werewolves was the hardest thing I ever did." He frowned, then glanced at me. "I say that, but every time I open a cage or break down a door to find werewolves in the most inhumane conditions, uniting the Hunters and werewolves so we can work together was also the best thing I ever did."

"How did your mother feel about you falling for a human?" I asked.

He smiled a patient smile and I realized another reason why so many looked up to him. He was never condescending or rude. He was patient, kind, and wanted everyone to be on the same page. His answer surprised me. "I forget you haven't met my mother. She's human."

I stared at him. "But you're an Alpha."

He nodded. "A fluke of nature." He grinned in a self-deprecating way. "Apparently someone figures I can make a difference even if it doesn't make sense."

"The werewolves at Lobotraz called you the guardian of werewolves."

The look of surprise on his face quickly swept into another grin. "That sounds a bit much, don't you think?"

I shook my head. "Honestly? I think it fits. I've never met anyone who makes as much of a difference as you do."

He dropped his gaze to the red sand. "I can never do enough. No matter how many werewolves I save, there are others out there being tortured and killed just because they can phase into a wolf." He glanced at me. "Having Nikki at my side makes it manageable. She helps me see that while I might not be able to save them all, I can try my best and it'll make a difference to each werewolf my team gives a new life."

I ran a hand through my hair to push it back from my face and asked the question that had been burning through my mind since I met Nora. "Can you truly be complete with a human?"

The smile he gave this time was heavy with experience. Sorrow and laughter warred in his eyes, and the honesty of his expression left no doubt in my mind. "Nikki is my night and day, my moon, my stars, and every driving force that keeps my lungs filling up with air and my heart beating to drive blood through my body so I can fight to make a difference. Without Nikki, I am not me." He met my eyes. "Choose the girl who makes you more because you are with her. It doesn't matter her race. All that matters is she does more than just completes you, she brings out who you truly are."

# Chapter 19

I paced my quarters that night, unable to sleep. Mom's crew had done their job. The new center was spotless and ready for habitation, and the werewolves and Hunters from Jaze's team that helped out left without a word. Werewolves from Lobotraz took up the various rooms, each one full of as much good food as they could eat and sleeping in the luxuries of down comforters, thick robes, and soft cotton pajamas.

The comforts that lulled them to sleep had the opposite effect on me. I couldn't relax in the fine surroundings with the thought of Nora trapped in her father's grasp. I felt pent up and caged, but nothing held me in except the fact that I had nowhere else to go. I paced the room so many times I wondered that there was no groove where my feet walked.

The phone rang and I jumped for it. "Did you find her?" I couldn't keep the hope out of my voice.

Mom took a breath. "I'm sorry, son, but there's word-"

All of my emotions that had been roiling beneath the surface came to a head. "What good is money if it can't find her?" I yelled into the phone. I threw it across the room and it broke into pieces next to the open door.

Gem watched me with lifted eyebrows from the doorway, her blue gaze barely fazed. "That's how you talk to your mother?"

A pang of guilt ran through me. Gem had been looking for her own parents, and she hadn't given up hope that they were still searching for her, that it was only a matter of time until they found each other, and here I was acting ungrateful toward my own mother who was very much in touch and as parentally relieved that I was still alive as I could imagine her being.

"Not usually," I muttered, refusing to meet her eyes.

Gem picked up the bigger pieces of the phone and came

over to the couch. She sat down lightly and tucked her bare feet underneath her. She held out the pieces. "You need to apologize."

"The phone's broken," I said stubbornly.

She rolled her eyes and dumped the pieces into my lap. "Don't take the easy way out. You'll regret it."

I wanted to argue, but it took one look at her determined gaze, her petite arms striped with Rob's black lashes, her pixie cut rebellious pink hair, and her blue eyes much older than her sixteen years, and I couldn't help but remember her passing over the cup of water through silver bars and the faith she had that she would be rescued, a faith that had carried me when my own soul was lost. My heart leaped at her nearness and gratitude for all she had done filled my chest. I would have died if it wasn't for her care, and I couldn't argue with her now.

"Fine."

"Great!" She jumped to her feet. "When are we leaving?"

I eyed her suspiciously. "We?"

She nodded. "I don't trust you to make a good apology by yourself. It sounds like you need help with these things, and I've got nothing else to do until my parents are found."

Her tone begged me not to leave her at the rehab center with the other broken werewolves. I sighed. It was the least I could do. "Fine."

She grinned and led the way out the door. I was tempted to point out that it was almost midnight, but she was already halfway down the hall. I sighed again in exasperation and followed her. I wanted to forget my conversation with Jaze and just enjoy being with her. The energy that surrounded Gem made me feel younger, like the days we had survived together were only a dream. I laughed as she skipped down the hall, my tiny sprite full of fire.

"Are you coming?" she asked when she reached the door.

She gazed up at me, her blue eyes reflecting the light of the moon, and my breath caught in my throat. No matter what Jaze went through with Nikki, he hadn't had to look on such a warm, carefree face and try to convince himself he wasn't in love.

***

"This is fancy," Gem said, her eyes wide as I passed through the gate and drove down the tree-lined driveway to my parents' mansion.

"Cold and lifeless in its own sort of way," I said softly.

She shot me a glance, but didn't comment. Her mouth fell open when a servant in a tuxedo came out to open the door.

"Good to see you back, Master Vance," James said. His brown hair was streaked with gray and blue eyes were now spectacled with fine lines at the corners.

"Good to see you, too, James," I replied. My chest had grown tighter with every foot down the driveway. It was hard to breathe past the knot in my throat at the familiar, aged faces of the servants who were once my only companions peering from the doorway. I swallowed and led the way up the eight white steps to the gilded front doors tall enough to allow entrance to an ogre.

Pat met us at the door, pretending to hold it open with a white-gloved hand even though we both knew the lion's-claw door stopper really did the work. "Splendid to see you," he said. His Irish accent was more faded than I remembered.

"Thank you, same to you," I said honestly. "I've missed everyone."

"We've missed you, sir," Rosemary, the woman who had once been more of a mother to me than my own mom said with a sincerity that shone in her soft brown eyes. "It's so good to have you back. How long will you be staying?"

"Just an hour or so." The understanding and regret in her gaze ate at my heart, but I could barely stand to pass through the doorway, much less stay longer in the house than necessary.

"Madam is through here," Jerry said, leading the way.

Light played off the top of his head that had once held hair, at least as far as my younger self remembered. His stature held dignity and grace, but his steps were slower and his shoulders bowed at an angle that hadn't been there when I was small.

"Been a long couple of years?" I asked as nonchalantly as possible. Gem walked beside me, pausing now and then to study the paintings Mom collected and the fine tapestries Dad traded for overseas. She fell behind, then rushed to catch up with staccato beats of bare feet. She looked like she regretted not wearing shoes. I wanted to tell her it would give the servants something to do besides cater to my parents' every whim, but I decided to keep things at a low roar as long as I could.

"It's definitely been interesting," Jerry replied in a tone that revealed nothing. He glanced at me, but when I met his gaze he dropped his eyes and fell silent.

"I'm not a child anymore," I said quietly. "You can tell me what's been going on. It's obvious everyone's been run ragged."

"It's not my place to say, Master Vance," he replied, his eyes straight ahead.

I gritted my teeth and we followed him through two more sets of doors to Mom's favorite sitting room. Our feet sunk into red plush carpet and a sigh of contentment escaped from Gem. She threw me an embarrassed look, but being absent from the mansion for thirteen years had also dampened my memory of the grandeur of the rooms. Two had been stark and bleak compared to the gold-gilded white walls, the intricate scroll work on the mahogany furniture, and the fake fire in the fireplace that danced without giving off heat.

Mom sat in a day lounge by the fire, her velvet-slippered feet resting on a white cushion while she read a book with a muscle-bound man on the cover. She looked up at our entrance and her face paled an instant before she rose and rushed over.

"My goodness, Vance. Why didn't you tell me you were paying a visit?" she asked, her tone strange. She put her arms around me in an awkward hug, her hands fluttering at my back like a pair of doves trying to escape.

"I, uh, thought it'd be okay to stop by," I said, stumbling over my words in a way I never did. Mom's embrace, though clumsy, did more to remind me of her love than a thousand phone calls. I didn't realize how much I had missed it. Nora's voice whispered in my head that I did know, I had just shoved it down behind a wall of anger and resentment camouflaged in indifference. The need to hear the words from her lips rushed through me with a longing ache.

"Of course it's okay," Mom said, stepping back. Her hands quivered in front of her until she locked her fingers and stood in a semblance of composure. She noticed Gem for the first time. "Oh, and who is this?"

Gem stepped forward before I could introduce her and shook Mom's hand. "Just Gem. I'm here for moral support."

I shot her a look, but she pretended not to notice.

Mom's brows drew together. "Moral support?" Worry touched her brown eyes that were a shade darker than mine.

I looked at the ceiling, but didn't find any help there and sighed. "I owe you an apology for the way I spoke to you on the phone."

"And you threw the phone at the wall and it shattered," Gem put in helpfully.

I glared at her this time, but she merely smiled her sprite smile and waited for me to continue. I turned back to Mom. "And I rudely hung up."

Gem sputtered, but I ignored her.

A smile of understanding touched Mom's lips. "Oh, darling, you don't have to apologize. You're so worried about

Nora. I would never hold anything like that against you."

Her comment brought an ironic smile to the corners of my mouth. "Need I remind you that you wanted me to kill her when I first found her?"

She laughed and sounded very much like the mother I was used to arguing with over the phone. "Semantics, Vance, dear. She is a Hunter's daughter and I didn't want you to get hurt."

"So why the change of heart?" I pressed.

She shrugged, but the lightness of the action was belied by her forced smile. "It's obvious that you've come to care about her very much, despite the fact that she's human." The last word came out of her mouth liked it tasted bad.

"Being human doesn't make her less than we are, Mother," I said with a touch of bite to my tone.

"You keep telling yourself that," my mother replied quickly. She glanced at Gem, then forced another smile to her face. "How is the new rehabilitation center coming along?"

"It's done," Gem said before flitting away like a ballerina to take a closer look at the fire.

Mom nodded. "They do work quickly. I hear you have Jaze helping you."

"It's really the other way around," Gem said. "Jaze has all the help he needs; we just try to stay busy." She shot me a triumphant look and I rolled my eyes.

Mom searched for something to say and settled on, "Your father will be home soon. Perhaps we can have dinner together."

The thought of Dad sent a sharp pain through my chest. I gave Mom a searching look and she dropped her eyes. We both knew Dad could care less about whether I was home for dinner. I turned to the door. "I'll be going. It's just, well, I'm sorry about the way I spoke to you." Gem cleared her throat daintily and I grimaced. "And about breaking the phone. You deserve more respect than that."

"Thank you, Vance," Mom said.

She made no move to stop me. Gem skipped back to my side and Jerry opened the door for us to leave, but Mom spoke at the last moment. "Vance?"

I turned slowly; the knowledge that the visit had gone just how I knew it would sat heavily in my chest. "Yes, Mother?"

Her voice revealed nothing. "I'm glad you came to visit."

I watched her for a second, wondering if she had any regrets, but no tears glittered in the firelight, her hands now held her book firmly again, and she stood by the day lounge chair as if ready to take up where she had left off. I pushed down the emotions that rose unbidden and nodded. "It was nice to see you." I left through the door and Jerry pulled it shut behind us.

***

"Who would have thought someone like you could have come from all that?" Gem mused aloud on our way back to Two.

"You mean the money?" I hazarded as I turned the jeep onto one of the many trails in the red rocks.

"I mean the cold shoulder. Your butlers showed more heart at seeing you than your mom. How long has it been since you were last there?"

I forced an indifferent tone. "Thirteen years. I moved to Two when I was six."

She whistled, then stuck her bare feet on the dash. "Well, when we find my parents you can meet them and see how real parents are supposed to act."

That struck too close to the surface. "At least I know where my parents are," I shot back. Gem fell silent and I immediately regretted the statement. I let out a sigh. "I'm sorry, Gem. I shouldn't take out my frustrations on you. You don't deserve it."

A smile touched her lips and her blue eyes sparkled. "That's alright. I know you don't mean it." She fell silent, then said, "It was a beautiful house, though."

I rolled my eyes. "Like I said, what good is money if you can't use it to get what you want most?"

She sat in silence for a few minutes, then I saw her smile out of the corner of my eye. "What?" I asked.

Her smile turned to a grin. "When they first threw you in that cage, I didn't take you for the practical type."

"Oh really? What did you take me for, the beaten and bleeding type?" I asked with heavy sarcasm that made her smile even bigger.

She shook her head. "The considerate type. You have sincere eyes."

That took me back. I opened my mouth to give a retort, but none came. "Thanks," I said after a minute.

She gave me another smile and wiggled her feet on the dash. "You're welcome." She turned up the radio and began to sing off-key to a country song about horses and rain.

About an hour into our drive, her head lolled against my shoulder and her breathing slowed. The trust she showed me soothed the burned edges of my heart and I drove carefully to avoid jarring her awake.

She slept for a half hour when her muscles tightened and a yell tore from her lips. She stared unseeing at the land around us, her eyes lost in her nightmare. I pulled over quickly and put my arms around her. Her body shook like a leaf and I felt her bones through her skin, reminding me of how frail she was. "It's alright, Gem. It's just a dream. We're not in Lobotraz anymore," I breathed into her hair.

She took several deep breaths, then held me with her surprising strength. "It was horrible," she said, her voice soft and weak with fear. "He wouldn't stop hurting me. I told him everything I knew, but he wouldn't stop."

Tears soaked my shirt and I held her close. "I know," I said. "But it's over now. You'll never have to go back there."

She looked up at me, pain and terror in her eyes. "Promise?"

I nodded. "I promise."

She buried her head against my chest and the sobs that shook her body brought tears to my eyes. I closed them and felt the sorrow, fear, and desperation that made up those long days in Lobotraz well up in my chest. I forced it down and focused on Gem, rubbing a hand down her back and talking quietly until her sobs slowed. She eventually fell back into an exhausted sleep and I drove us slowly to the rehabilitation center. The fact that neither of us had a home to go to after all we had experienced at Lobotraz struck hard and I regretted my visit with my mom even more.

# Chapter 20

"Need a break?" Jaze asked after I set Gem gently in her bed and shut the door.

I turned to see him waiting down the hall with a pack in one hand. "What do you have in mind?" I asked. The thought of getting away from the walls and the scent of recovering werewolves was welcome.

"I have a team following the first lead we've found. Until we hear from them, we're sitting tight." He tipped his head to indicate the walls and the scent of fresh paint that emanated from them. "Some of us wait better outdoors."

"Lead the way," I said. "My thoughts are so jumbled I might send us off a cliff."

He laughed and glanced back at me. "I prefer to avoid cliffs if at all possible."

I grinned and followed him through the doors to find Jet and Kaynan waiting for us. Kaynan handed me a pack and we strode out across the desert, the night air cooling as it drove the heat of the day from the sand.

We left the red rocks behind and crossed sand dunes spotted with sage and the occasional cactus. The fresh air was filled with scents of jackrabbits, snakes, and lizards taking advantage of the last vestiges of warmth before the night turned cold. After a short distance, Jaze knelt and untied his shoes. He knotted the laces together and slipped them through a loop in his pack so he could walk barefoot. Kaynan and Jet did the same.

Jaze caught my eye with a smile. "Can't say you don't have some things figured out," he said, pushing his feet into the warm sand.

I shrugged. "The fewer clothes out here, the better."

Kaynan lifted an eyebrow. "Whoa now, we need to draw a line somewhere."

We laughed and I nodded. "I didn't say there weren't some downfalls to the situation."

Jet took a deep breath and turned his face to the rising moon. It was only a quarter full, but the brush of it across my face stilled the confusion in my heart like nothing else had been able to do. The others fell silent and for a moment we were four individuals linked by a related affinity to the moon. I regretted taking Gem inside. I should have let her sleep in the jeep, bathed in moonlight. We continued on and my thoughts turned to both girls. They were so different, and the hold they had on me so completely diverse that I couldn't compare them.

I concentrated on the landscape, losing myself in the waves of sand underfoot. It looked like we walked across a still, moonlit ocean, the waves frozen in soft curves that accentuated the rise and fall of the dunes. Kaynan jumped when a scorpion scurried away from the base of a cactus disturbed by his footfalls nearby. "I think we should put our shoes back on," the red-eyed werewolf said warily, his eyes on the creature.

Jet laughed, surprising us all. "Afraid of bugs," he said in a tone laced with humor.

Kaynan glowered at him. "They can kill you with their stingers," he argued.

The light in Jet's dark blue eyes danced. "And you're defenseless?"

Kaynan grumbled something about deadly creatures who didn't respect the dangers of a knife, but he didn't put his shoes back on. Jet continued to smile, the light of the moon softening the hardened edge I was use to seeing from him. He was like a different person away from the dangers and pain of the other werewolves. It was like for a moment, he was allowing himself just to exist under the midnight sky. I tried to do the same and found myself appreciating the feeling of walking with three trusted companions with no worry of being jumped or fought for leadership. It was strange to find Alphas so comfortable with each other, a rare thing that I appreciated even more for having lived at Two.

Jaze stopped us near a dead, twisted tree that had long ago succumbed to the desert heat. We lounged in the sand and he pulled out a bag of marshmallows and graham crackers.

"S'mores?" I asked, surprised. Roasting marshmallows felt a bit trivial after all we had been through.

He tipped his head to indicate my bag. I opened it and found several small logs. Jet dumped out the same and Kaynan built them into a teepee for a fire. He shoved newspaper and tinder scraps from the construction underneath, then lit it on fire with a lighter. I sat back and enjoyed the warm flicker that bathed the sand around the fire in rosy orange. The hum of the night insects sounded fuller somehow with the light of the fire coloring the edges of the darkness.

Kaynan broke several sticks from the dried tree and used his knife to whittle the ends to a point. "Where did that come from?" I asked, curious.

He glanced at the knife, then looked back at me. "Do you remember Mouse, the scrawny werewolf from the house who's good with computers?" At my nod, he smiled. "He made this for me as a thank you gift for saving his life."

My eyebrows rose and Jaze said, "Tell it straight. You took a bullet for him. It was one of the bravest things I've ever seen."

Kaynan shook his head. "I've seen braver," he replied in a tone that indicated they involved the other werewolves around the fire. He pushed something on the blade and the knife edges slid back into the silver band to form a straight, thin bar. He hit the bar on his wrist and it wrapped around, creating a solid wristband that appeared to not have any edges. He pushed on the spot again and it opened, then the blades appeared.

"That's awesome," I said.

He nodded. "Mouse'll surprise you. Better watch out for that one."

"He might avoid you to death," Jet replied with a touch of humor.

"Jet," Jaze said in a tone of surprise.

Kaynan glanced at me. "Mouse is the most loyal werewolf you'll ever find. Jaze is the only one who holds his loyalty."

"Justly deserved," Jet said quietly. "I admire him."

All of us looked at the black-haired werewolf in surprise. His dark blue eyes shone with a light of humility. "He's taught me the worth of loyalty," he said quietly, his eyes on the fire.

We fell silent and Jaze handed out the marshmallows to go with Kaynan's sticks. I held mine over the fire and turned it slowly, watching the white flesh turn golden brown and then black in the heat of the flames. Memories of Two glowing red and gold against the sunset flooded my mind. I blinked against the surge of emotion that strove to chase away the quiet peace I found sitting by the fire.

"I think it's done," Kaynan said.

My eyes focused and I realized my marshmallow had been reduced to a pitiful black lump that no longer held even the interest of the lapping flames. I laughed and scrapped it off with another stick, then accepted a new marshmallow from Jaze. "Guess I'd better pay attention."

"Only if you actually want to make a s'more," Jaze replied.

"Charcoal does come in handy," Kaynan said. He set a square of chocolate on his graham cracker, then pressed his perfectly golden brown marshmallow down with another cracker. "But s'mores taste better." He held up his completed creation for everyone to see and was about to take a bite when Jet swiped it from his hand and had it in his mouth before the red-eyed werewolf could even blink.

He stared at Jet in astonishment. "That was impressive."

Jet gave a wide grin that revealed partially-chewed graham crackers and squishy marshmallow mixed with chocolate.

"Not that impressive," Kaynan said, pushing his shoulder.

Jet shut his mouth, but the grin on his face refused to leave. I had an impression that Jaze's team seldom had the chance to relax like this. They savored the moments as I did; all of us were reluctant to return to the problems that would come back when we reached the rehabilitation center. Jaze handled so much I wondered how he could relax at all.

I put my s'more together and took a bite, relishing the taste of the chocolate mixed with the roasted marshmallow and graham cracker. The feeling of being a young boy again trying to find his place in the world surfaced and I smiled. For now, it was enough to have a warm fire and good friends surrounding it. I looked up at the stars and saw the miracle Jaze spoke of in them. I glanced back and found him looking as well.

\*\*\*

A scent touched my nose when we reached the rehabilitation center. A werewolf dressed in black went to Jaze and they spoke quietly for a few minutes. The werewolf handed Jaze a small piece of paper, then disappeared into the night. Jaze's eyes met mine and my stomach tightened. "Our lead turned out to be right," he said. He waited until we reached the door, then handed me the piece of paper.

A foul scent touched my nose. "What is this?"

He watched me, his face carefully expressionless. "I took my team to the bodies you ran to the other night."

"Of the Hunters we killed?" I hazarded quietly.

He nodded. "I had a team search through them. Your werewolves were thorough about burning wallets and any identification, but this was found in a jacket."

He gestured to the piece of paper and I opened it. An address was written in a barely legible hand. A flicker of hope began to burn in my chest. I could scarcely bring myself to ask, "Where does it lead?"

He met my eyes, his brow creased. "An extremist Hunter training facility."

I stared at the address. If Ron was in charge of the Hunters, then we could find him through the facility. I would tear down every door and interrogate each person within those walls if I had to. It was the first thread of a chance to locate Nora, and Jaze's team had gone through the pockets of decaying bodies to discover it.

I swallowed the knot in my throat and held out a hand. "Thank you for finding this. I'll leave right away"

He stared at me a second, then shook my hand, a shadow of a smile touching his lips. "You're not going alone, you know."

"I figured as much," I replied.

He smiled and pulled the door open; it felt comforting to walk down the hall with a friend at my side once more.

\*\*\*

Footsteps rushed to meet us and I recognized the sound before Gem came into view, her face flushed and lit by a big smile that made her blue eyes glow. "Vance, Vance, I heard the news! That's so exciting! We're going to find her." She flew into my arms and gave me a tight hug, then she hugged Jaze as well. I would have laughed at the baffled expression on his face if it wasn't for the fact that I was still recovering from the news. I don't know how Gem had overheard, but being able to share it with her made it somewhat more manageable.

"It's the best lead we've got. It's got to take us somewhere," I replied.

"Of course it does," she agreed, beaming. "When are we going?"

I glanced at Jaze. "I don't think this is a safe expedition for you, Gem. You could get hurt."

A glimmer of ferocious tenacity sparkled in her eyes. "Don't think you can leave me out on this one, Vance. We've been through too much together. I want to see Rob go down as much as you do."

Jaze let out a breath and when I glanced at him, he shrugged as if to say the choice wasn't his.

I gave in. "Fine, but you've got to promise me that if it gets too dangerous, I can ask you to hang back."

Her hand slipped into mine. "Still protecting me from the world, Vance?" she asked with a hint of teasing to her tone.

"As much as I can," I replied.

I glanced over and saw Jaze watching us, but there was no judgment in his expression. I again appreciated his patience and understanding. "Let's get ready to go," I said quietly. Gem nodded and skipped off down the hallway toward her room.

"Can we protect her?" I asked Jaze in an undertone.

His brow creased. "After what she's been through, I doubt anything scares her. My team will keep her safe."

I thanked him and walked quickly to my room to make preparations. Gem appeared a few seconds later with a scantily packed bag and a pair of shoes hanging around her neck. At my look, she sighed, "You never know when you might need them."

I grinned and slipped mine on. "They're easier to wear than carry."

She hesitated, then followed my lead as though it was painful. I threw a few supplies into my pack, then straightened to find her watching me, her bright expression darkened by shadows that had nothing to do with the lighting in the room.

"They haven't found my parents yet," she said. "What if I've lost them forever?"

I shook my head. "There's no way they're not looking for you right now. There are just a lot of places to search." I felt foolish for saying it, but it must have been the right thing because tears filled her eyes.

"You're right, you know," she said with a tremor in her bubbly voice. "Jaze will find them. I know he will." A tear ran over and she wiped it away with another smile. "Look at me, falling apart before we go rescue Nora." She eyed me sternly. "You're supposed to be the stalwart one, remember? Not the one who reduces girls to mere blabbering babies."

A laugh escaped my lips. "Oh that's my role now, huh?"

She nodded in all seriousness, a touch of concern in her eyes. "Nora is safe, too, you know."

Her words tightened the pit in my stomach. "I sure hope so."

Gem touched my arm. "She is," she said with the faith that had carried me further than I cared to admit. "I just know she is. You can't give up until she's out of Rob's clutches. She'll be alright, I just know it."

"She's a strong person," I agreed.

She rose onto her tiptoes and kissed me on the nose. "Hang in there, Vance, my reluctant hero. You'll save the world yet."

I laughed and she danced on her toes. "We'd better get going."

I nodded and she ran out the door, then paused halfway down the hall to make sure I was coming. I checked that the few meager belongings I owned were put away, then followed her to the front door.

# Chapter 21

We pulled up to a small, brown-bricked security building that controlled the entrance to a fenced-in compound. The fence was twelve feet high and topped with razor-wire. A brick wall on the other side hid whatever was inside from view.

Jaze pulled up to the security building and rolled down his window. A black-tinted pane of glass slid open to reveal two humorless officials in dark green uniforms.

"Sorry, kid, but you missed the museum about twenty minutes back," the first officer said in a tone that indicated we weren't the first strangers to show up at his window, he just didn't know we were the first to arrive on purpose.

"Really?" Jaze glanced at Jet with a lifted eyebrow. "How could we have missed it?"

Jet shrugged, his eyes on the officers.

Jaze lifted his gun and shot both men in the neck with tranquilizer darts before they could sound an alert. He set the gun back down and met my eyes in the rear-view mirror. "The museum would probably have less security."

I rolled my eyes and he chuckled. Jet slipped out the door, his dark eyes glittering as though he lived for breaking and entering into hostile compounds. Gem leaned against my arm as the werewolf silently tripped the lock for the door and disappeared inside. A few seconds later, the gate slid open in front of us. Jet appeared at the passenger door like a wraith, a half-smile on his face.

"What's up?" Jaze pressed.

"Cameras," Jet said in his brief way. "You'll find this interesting."

Jaze gave him a doubtful look, but pulled slowly through the gate. "Which way?" he asked.

"Left," I replied. Mouse had somehow printed out an

aerial view of the compound despite the fact that its existence was left out of every major satellite view of the area that I could find. I had suspicions that he used a government satellite for the shot. When I thanked him, he acted like he didn't know what I was talking about, then he handed me a security key card to use inside the compound and he couldn't hide his small smile no matter how hard he looked at the floor.

"Take a right here," I whispered. Floodlights that towered above us lit every inch of the road. I knew it was only a matter of time before the unauthorized truck was spotted. The thought of finding information that might lead to Rob or Nora sent a sharp pain through my chest. I wouldn't give up any advantage we could gain.

"There's storage to the left. We might be able to hide the vehicle there," Gem suggested, leaning over the map next to me.

Jaze pulled under a three-sided storage shed filled with stacks of moldy hay bales. When we climbed out, the scent of fermenting greenery, opportunistic mice, and the arid smell of gunpowder filled my nose.

"Keep together," I whispered. Jaze, Gem, and Kaynan fell in behind me while Jet kept watch at the corner. I pulled out the photo. "This looks like the control center. I say we take the shortest route there, quick in and out."

"We could have interrogated the guards at the gate," Kaynan said. He adjusted the dark sunglasses he wore to hide his red eyes and gave me an apologetic shrug. "It might have saved us a headache."

Jaze shook his head. "No one tells the gate guards anything. They'd be a liability and Ron's been one step ahead since he got Nora back. Let's just hope he doesn't know we're coming."

Jet's expression said otherwise as he led the way across a

short stretch of asphalt and under an arch cut in a thick hedge.

The scent of blood colored the air with iron the further we walked. The next arch led us to a series of posts with small, flat boards nailed on top. The scent of day-old gunfire was unmistakable, and the feathers and chunks of wings and feet twenty-five paces away tainted the air with a mild scent of decay. By the blood marks on the ground and the surrounding bushes, the birds had been alive just before they were shot, and some even after.

A surge of pity ran through my chest that the creatures had died at Rob's hand. It felt silly to bemoan chickens, but I had vowed to save every life from Rob's clutches, and I was determined to include each walk of life in that vow.

We crept further down the hedge and came to a cement enclosure with a large, black, daunting gate at the entrance. A quick check showed the gate to be locked. We could scale it, but the more suspicious activities we performed, the more likely we were to catch someone's attention.

"I've got this," Kaynan said quietly. He slipped something into the lock, jiggled it, and the lock popped open with a faint click. The werewolf then slipped back behind Jaze and Jet, a touch of chagrin to his smile.

"Glad to see your skills put to good use," Jaze said without a hint of reproach.

"Nice to have a chance to use them," Kaynan replied evenly.

"I'm just happy I didn't have to break the gate down with my muscles," Gem said. She flexed, showing her pathetically skinny arms. "I'll save these babies for later."

The others laughed and I smiled at the sparkle in her eyes. She might have been the weakest of us, but she was still the bravest. I opened the gate and waited for the others to pass through, then shut it quietly behind us. The cement walls rose about ten feet high and stretched for a long distance before branching off. Several tunnels forked away from the main walkway.

"A maze, really?" Kaynan asked dryly.

"Original," Jet replied. His eyes glittered darkly. The way his gaze roamed the landscape and his muscles tensed as though he was ready to take down an army set me on edge.

Jaze looked at me and I gestured right. Going straight and turning left at the end was the quickest path, but it also went right past what looked like a guard station and I would rather be safe than sorry. We walked quickly down the cement walkway and I know I wasn't the only one who felt a little claustrophobic behind the tall walls. Gem slipped her hand into mine and I gave it a reassuring squeeze.

We passed one gap in the wall that led to an empty cement enclosure that smelled strongly of fear and werewolf blood. The next gap revealed chains on the ground, excrement, and more blood; the scent said that the recently missing inhabitants had been there a long time, suffering from wounds and neglect.

I gritted my teeth and Gem and I both passed the next gap without looking, but we heard sounds of disgust and exclamations from the others that matched the scent of death and decay in the air.

I led the others to the end of the row, then we turned and walked slowly down the back aisle. Fortunately, there were no more gaps in the cement wall. We waited at the exit of the maze until a rotating camera finished its path and turned back in the other direction, then we slipped past and crept through a small stand of trees to another enclosure.

The building showed as a black square on the map. Mouse had circled it and written coordinates on the right side in case we had any trouble reaching it. He said that was where all the electronic transmissions came from and guessed it was the central station for the training grounds. The building smelled of humans and I wondered how many we would find inside.

Two guards stood at the only door, assault rifles held loose in their hands and bored expressions on their faces. Jaze and Kaynan raised their guns, then Jaze counted quietly and they both pulled their triggers. Two darts flew through the air to land in the necks of both guards. One let out a soft exclamation, then they slumped to the ground.

We walked silently across the small cement clearing and I used the key card Mouse had given me to open the door while Jet and Kaynan pulled the bodies into the trees. They caught up to us inside. I folded the aerial picture, wishing we had a map of the inside but knowing we had gotten lucky so far. I pulled out my gun and took the right hall with Gem, Jaze and Jet took the middle, while Kaynan went down the left.

Our goal was to find someone in charge and interrogate them, then compare the information when we met back at the truck in fifteen minutes. It wasn't much time, but we figured any longer and we would risk bringing down the entire training facility to practice on our hides, though Jaze pointed out dryly that would definitely help us find Rob, just at the wrong end of his gun.

The building turned out to have more of a classroom setting than a control center. Gem and I passed four classrooms containing about twenty Hunters each. The thought sent chills through my body that there were so many extremists waiting to take down werewolves. I worried about the other members of our team and hoped they were being careful, then a loud hum sounded and the lights shut off.

The windowless building was pitch-black. Whoever had tripped the power apparently had shut off the back-up generators as well, because no emergency lighting showed.

Cries of alarm went up from the classrooms as Gem and I hurried past, their gray images and wide stares making both of us smile.

We followed the hallway to the left, then found a closed door with 'No Entrance' painted in big red letters on the outside. "Subtle," I said softly. Gem grinned and tried the door. It was locked. I gripped the handle in both hands and turned it sharply to the right. A pop sounded, then the door swung inward.

Flashlight beams bounced around the room as five or six men called out to each other, checking fuses, following wiring, and trying to get the cameras and computers back online. A man about six and a half feet tall stood at the back of the room giving orders. He didn't look as frantic as the rest, but I could smell the anxiety that flowed from him and knew he hid it well.

"Stay out here," I whispered to Gem. She nodded, her eyes wide.

I stepped into the room and followed the wall so I could crouch behind the desks if they shone their lights in my direction. I was almost to the man when shots rang out. I froze, then saw Kaynan stand with his hands up. All six of the men had their flashlights trained on him. Blood trickled from Kaynan's shoulder and I wondered if they used silver bullets. The fact that this was a Hunter training facility made the possibility very likely. We didn't have much time to get the bullet out.

I crossed the remaining ground to the leader quickly, then wrapped an arm around his neck and jabbed my gun into his ribs. "Call them off," I warned him in a low growl.

His muscles tensed and I thought for a moment that he would fight me, then he let out a breath and said, "Drop your guns."

"But Chief," one of the men protested; he shut up when

he saw that his commander was at gunpoint. All guns dropped to the ground and Jet collected them with a gleam of satisfaction in his eyes.

Jaze escorted the other five men from the room and left Jet to guard them. When he returned, I had the Chief in a chair with his hands tied behind his back and my gun pointed casually at his chest.

I felt the seconds tick away before we got the bullet out of Kaynan's bleeding shoulder. "You should get that looked at," I said.

"It's alright," the Alpha replied. He rolled his shoulder and winced. "At least, it's not going to kill me anytime soon."

"But it's probably silver," I pointed out. "Is that a risk you're willing to take?"

He gave me an assessing look, his red eyes calm. "Silver doesn't affect me the way it does the rest of you. I'll be fine."

"Nonetheless," Jaze said. "You should put some pressure on the wound so you don't bleed to death. Dying would really put a damper on our mission, and I don't want to explain to Grace that her stubborn boyfriend refused to take care of himself."

Kaynan chuckled and accepted a waded up cloth Gem wordlessly handed him. He turned away to tend to his wound. I leaned against the desk by the Chief and studied him carefully.

The man wore a dark blue dress jacket over a black shirt, matching dark blue pants, and shoes that looked like they had never been scuffed in their life. His hair was black and slicked back, and he wore thin glasses that now sat askew on his nose. He regarded me calmly, though a slight hint of fear mixed with his bran muffin and aftershave scent. I decided to press my advantage.

"We're werewolves," I began without preamble. "All of us, and there are more werewolves and *actual*," I stressed the last word, "Hunters on their way. We're looking for Rob and I know you have information that will lead us to him."

The Chief's eyes tightened, but he gave no effort to answer me. I looked over at Jaze and shrugged. "Looks like we'll have to bite him."

"Bite him?" Jaze's eyebrows rose, but he played along. "Don't you think that's going a bit far?"

I smiled a predatory smile. "When he turns into a werewolf, he'll have to answer because we're Alphas."

The Chief's face had gone pale at the mention of getting bit. I placed a lot of faith in the lie, but knowing Rob, he would feed his extremists with as much bunk about werewolves as he could to make them want to kill us that much more.

He shook his head. "Don't bite me, please. I have a family."

"It's not that bad," I pressed, drawing closer to him. "One bite and you'll be hunted for the rest of your life. Your family will never be safe."

His face paled further and he finally said, "What do you want to know?"

Jaze met the Chief's eyes. "We need to know where we can find Rob."

The Chief shook his head quickly. "I'll tell you anything but that, anything at all. It's just, well, he'll-"

"He'll kill you if he finds out you sent a pack of werewolves to attack him?" I guessed.

He nodded, his watery eyes worried.

I held out a hand. "Where's your wallet?"

He hesitated, his eyes flicking from Jaze to me. I lifted my eyebrows slightly. The Chief nodded at the desk behind us and I found a brown leather wallet in the top drawer. I pulled out his driver's license and checked the address. "Look at it this way. You can either tell us what we need to know and go back home to your family," I gave him an honest smile, "And I promise if you tell us what we need to know, you and your men will leave here with your lives, and after we have Rob you won't have to worry about anyone coming after you." My gaze darkened. "But if you don't tell us, I have no choice but to bite or shoot you and your men because I can't have you running to Rob and telling him we're on his trail."

I raised my gun and aimed it at the center of his forehead. I hoped he didn't notice the point of the dart protruding from the end. His eyes met mine and I held his gaze. He finally sighed and nodded. I lowered my gun. "Just remember," I said in a tone that left no room for argument. "What you tell us must be the truth, because if you lie and more innocent werewolves are hurt at Rob's hand before we have the chance to stop him, then you're family will always be in danger. I've never lost a trail, and I will find you."

He swallowed, then met my serious gaze. "I'll tell you the truth." At my nod, he continued, "He's holed up in a house in Mancos, Colorado. Go to fourteen-fourteen Old Mill Road."

Getting the exact address surprised me. "How do you know he's there for sure?"

The Chief gave a chagrined shrug. "The house belongs to a prominent supporter of the Hunters."

"Extremist Hunters," Kaynan said.

I untied the Chief's hands and stepped back. He rose uneasily to his feet and rubbed his wrists. "I'm free to go? Just like that?"

I nodded. "We're not vicious killers, no matter what garbage Rob feeds you."

"But let me remind you one thing," Jaze said. He took a step toward the Chief and the man backed a step away. "If you are being honest, and I feel that you are, you just told us the address of your boss' location. If you sound an alarm after we leave this facility and tell Rob what happened, he will undoubtedly kill you and possibly your entire family for the information you gave." He glanced at me. "And there's no doubt in my mind that he will draw out your death so it's painful and agonizing."

The Chief's face blanched and he nodded quickly. "I've been thinking about taking up farming," he said. I was surprised to hear that he was being honest. "It would be a good way to leave this all behind."

"An excellent idea," Jaze agreed. He held out his hand. The Chief hesitated, then shook it. He shook mine, too, then we joined Jet at the doorway and left. I tossed the Chief's wallet in a garbage can near the front door. Jaze glanced at me but didn't say anything. We exited the building to find Jaze's Hunters and werewolves swarming the training facility. It was odd how reassuring I found the small wolf paw print they wore on their hats and uniforms. Jaze gave his orders to shut down the facility, then we crossed back to the jeep and left the Hunter training grounds feeling as though we had truly accomplished something.

# Chapter 22

The address led us to a sweeping house on a hill in the beautiful Colorado countryside. The hope that I would soon be reunited with Nora made the crisp night air smell that much sweeter as we walked softly through the underbrush about a quarter of a mile from the house. Jaze's Hunters had staked out the place since we spoke to the Chief, and they reassured us that Rob was there and apparently unaware of our pending take-over.

"Senator Braken's house. I still can't believe it," Kaynan said, peering down the hill at the well-lit yellow-paneled, white-shuttered sprawling manor amid bushes, carefully manicured trees, and vast expanses of trimmed lawns that would make a stealthy approach difficult. To top it off, cameras swept every angle of the yard, rotating so that their views intersected and no shadow was left unsurveyed.

"Makes sense," Jaze replied quietly. "He's always stood in the way of the government helping werewolves. We should look up several of his supporters and see if they're in some way connected with Rob as well. I know a few agencies that'll be interested if they're compromised."

"That's a great idea," Kaynan replied, then, "Charlie wasn't kidding when he said the place was tight."

Jaze turned to Mouse. "Where's the electrical access to the house?"

Mouse pointed, his small computer already out and two cables ready. We followed him to a spot not too far from the house and hidden in a stand of trees. Kaynan and Jet began to dig with the small shovels they had brought from the jeep while Jaze, Gem, and I kept watch. They pulled up the wires and Mouse clipped his cables to them.

"Finished," Mouse said a second before all of the lights went out, bathing the house in darkness. "I estimate five minute before they start the generators."

"It'll be enough," Jaze replied. "Thanks."

They shot two guards with tranquilizer darts at the northeast corner of the house, then we crept around to the back where a wide deck was guarded by five more guards armed this time with what appeared to be grenades and submachine guns no doubt loaded with silver bullets.

"You got this?" Jaze whispered.

It took me a minute to realize he was talking to Gem and me; he, Jet, and Kaynan all had guards lined up in their sights.

"Vance, take the second to last one on the right; Gem, you take the last," Jaze whispered. He lifted his gun and we barely had a chance to aim before he whispered, "Fire."

I squeezed the trigger gently and saw a dart bloom from the neck of my guard. All five men fell to the deck with thumps loud enough that I worried someone would overhear. I glanced at Gem and she gave me a wide-eyed look, but her hands held her gun steady. We waited for a moment, but when no one showed up, we jumped over the deck railing and Jaze slowly opened the sliding door. He slipped into the dark dining hall and the rest of us followed. Gem slipped her hand into mine and I led her through the darkness after Jaze's team.

My heart gave a leap at Nora's scent permeating the air, the carpet, and everywhere I turned. The scent was days old in the dining room, but grew stronger as we went down the hall. A guard stepped in from a side door and Jet took him down with a sleeper hold before the man could make a sound. His eyes gleamed in the darkness and he stalked as gracefully as a hunting cat from one door to the next, his hands opening and closing into fists as though he could barely wait for the next attack.

Kaynan followed closely behind to flank Jet on one side while Jaze took the other. Jet acted as though he led with his nose instead of his eyes, and when Nora's scent grew stronger behind a door that led to the basement, he gestured to make sure I didn't miss it.

"I'm going after Nora," I whispered to Jaze. "You guys find Rob. She won't be safe until he's out of the picture."

"Take Gem and Kaynan," Jaze replied, his eyes on the dark hallway. "Mouse will send the alert when our backup arrives."

I nodded and Kaynan turned the doorknob silently. When it refused to budge, he put a bit more pressure behind it and the locked slipped with a quiet pop. A small red light started flashing above us.

I looked at Jaze. "The generators must be on," he whispered. "They know we're here. We've got to hurry."

I led the way down the stairs with Gem and Kaynan close behind. The stairs creaked with each step and the noise multiplied in my ears until it sounded like we were a marching band instead of three soft-footed werewolves. Nora's scent grew stronger and fresher the further we went down. We reached the bottom to find the basement sectioned into three long rooms. Rob's scent was fresh in the air, but so was the soft vanilla and sunflower aroma that made my heart thump loudly in my chest.

I hurried into the room on the left. It was dark, but emergency lighting flickered above, playing havoc with my werewolf eyesight. I peered between rows of boxes and crates and found a silver cage pushed against the far wall. A form was curled on the bottom.

My heart slowed and I took a careful step forward; my soul screamed for me to run to her and make sure she was alright. My mind argued back that Rob had killed her because of our relationship. A board creaked under my foot and the form stirred. My heart began to beat again.

"Nora?"

"Vance?" She sat up and peered through the darkness. "Vance, it's a trap," she said, horror thick in her voice.

I ran to the cage and pulled the door off in one quick jerk, then she was gathered in my arms, safe against my chest and away from the pains of a world she was too good for. She shook in my arms, her body more fragile than I remembered.

Gem pulled my arm. "Vance, they're behind us."

Shots rang out and Kaynan let out a growl before he phased and took down two guards with guns. Gem shot two with darts, then Kaynan grappled a third, pulling him down to the ground with his teeth sunk into the man's gun hand.

"Vance!" Gem called.

I turned in time to see a door I hadn't noticed behind the cage open and four more guards come through. "Stay behind me," I told Gem. "Watch over her." The blue-eyed werewolf nodded, her jaw set with fierce determination.

I set Nora gently down in a gap between two crates. "We'll protect you," I promised. Her beautiful green eyes held mine for a brief second before Gem stepped in to guard her.

I turned and found the guards almost to us. I crossed the floor and threw a punch at the first man's chest. He flew back into another guard, effectively blocking the door for a brief moment while I dealt with the other two. I ducked under a punch, then blocked a crowbar aimed for my head. I wanted to phase, but it was easier to protect the others in human form, so I gritted my teeth and settled into a boxing stance.

I jabbed one man in the face and felt his nose break under my knuckles, then hit him with a hook across the jaw that sent him spinning into the other man. Three men at the door managed to push their way in. All three had silver knives and I wondered if they were under orders not to shoot around Nora, though I doubted a man who would put his own daughter in a cage as a trap had any scruples.

The instinct to protect the two girls behind me rushed like fire through my veins. No one would hurt the girls I loved. Red rage filled my vision. A man tried to stab me with his knife. I caught his arm and pulled him forward into my fist. He collapsed motionless to the ground. I turned and found another man trying to get past me. I picked him up by his shoulder and leg, then threw him into the wall. He hit with a loud bang and fell to the floor. Another tried to reach Gem and Nora. I bent down and grabbed his foot, then swung him around and into the floor so hard the other guards stared at me, expressions of surprise and horror on their faces as the man lay motionless at my feet. I lifted my lips in a silent snarl, daring them to come forward.

Several attacked at the same time. I picked up a crate and smashed it on top of the first one, then backhanded the next one so hard he spun completely around before falling motionless to the ground. The crowbar slammed into my right side. I felt things tear internally, but the adrenaline and the rage that filled me at the thought that someone would hurt those I cared about covered it all in a red fog of fury. I grabbed my attacker by the throat and slammed him back against the wall. His eyes rolled up and he slid to the ground.

A guard sliced at my shoulder. I grabbed his wrist just below the knife and wrenched his arm down. He let out a yell of pain and held his dislocated shoulder. I threw a straight punch to his face and he staggered back into the men behind him, slowing them down. Gem fired darts behind me and took down two men fighting to get through the door. I kicked one man's knees out from under him, then drove my elbow into his sternum. His ribs caved in under the force of my blow and he gasped for air.

The crowbar connected with the back of my head and lights flashed in front of my eyes. One of the guards tried to get to Nora and Gem behind me and his shadow caught my eye. Gem grappled with him, her tiny figure the only thing between the man and Nora. He hit Gem in the face. A roar of rage filled my chest and I turned and grabbed him, then threw him at an overturned desk so hard one of the table legs when through his chest.

A man bull-rushed me and slammed me backward into one of the crates. The crate shattered beneath me in a mess of broken wood and metal bands. He picked up a wooden stake and tried to drive it through my heart. I kicked out and caught him in the stomach. When he doubled over, I lunged to my feet and slammed an uppercut into his jaw. His head whipped back and he fell over backwards.

"That's vampires, idiot," I growled, tossing the stake on top of him.

A guard tried to kick my legs out from under me. The kick barely moved me and I glared at him. His eyes widened and he took a step backwards. I turned and horse-kicked the guard in the chest, sending him sprawling into two men fighting Kaynan with double sets of knives. The red-eyed werewolf shot me a look of gratitude, then his eyes widened. I looked behind me to see more guards spilling out into the close quarters.

I glanced at Nora and Gem. Nora sat on the floor between the boxes with her legs pulled up and her eyes wide as she met mine. Fear tangled with her beautiful scent, and I wanted more than anything to carry her away from all of the violence and gore. Gem's blue eyes met my gaze with confidence that said she knew the odds we faced and was ready to take whatever was coming. She stood beside me and shot two more darts into the guards. "I'm out," she said quietly, her voice firm.

"We're going to be alright," I replied.

The man with the crowbar stepped forward and brought the bar back as another man swung at my stomach. I ignored the punch and caught the crowbar with my left hand, then ripped it from the man's hands. I spun and hit both the men with it hard enough to drop them both. More guards piled into the room. I glanced up and saw others coming down the stairs toward Kaynan. The sheer bulk of them would take us down, but I wouldn't give up without fighting for the girls who needed me.

I turned back to meet the rush when a black-haired shadow flowed through the door. A knife flashed and two guards fell. Two others yelled, then they were on their knees. Jet moved from one guard to the next, his knife a bare shard of silver before the men were down gasping out the last of their life blood. The look in the werewolf's eyes was dark and animalistic, cold and calculating as he judged his opponents and took them down without mercy. Memories flowed through his dark blue irises and he gritted his teeth as he took down another with a slice across the neck.

I was stunned at his grace and ruthless proficiency. Before I could move, half of the guards that came through the back door were down. The rest pressed forward as if sensing the menace that came behind them. Jet jumped against the wall, grabbed a rafter, and swung down to land in front of them. A snarl ripped from his throat and the guards backed up. Jet launched into them, his blade so quick four fell before I even saw them hit. The rest surged back against the door, but more guards were trying to come in. The group turned with the realization of their fate bright in their eyes.

I broke my gaze from the lethal assault that followed and turned to meet the attackers on our other side in time to block another slice with a knife. I picked up the guard and threw him into those behind him. They fell back into Kaynan, shaking off the two men that held him so another could stick him with a knife. Kaynan's teeth flashed and another fell to the ground.

Two guards rushed me while a third tried to sneak around to get the girls. I grabbed both men by the throat and smashed them to the ground with enough force to make the floor tremble. I then turned and grabbed the other guard by the collar before he could reach Gem and Nora. The man jabbed at my eye with his knife. I grabbed his arm and threw him in the air. He hit the ceiling and crashed down with plaster falling on top of him.

Jet ghosted to my side, the blade of his knife dark red and an edge of steel to his eyes that sent a surge of gratitude through me that he was on our side. He turned without a word and we faced the guards that made it past Kaynan. I picked the crowbar up and hefted the cold metal in my hands, levering it to take down as many as I could. A voice called down from the top of the stairs.

"Hold it," Jaze growled in a voice laced with iron and teeth, an Alpha bark that not even the guards could ignore. Everyone turned to see the werewolf with a gun to Rob's head. "Put down your weapons, now," Jaze commanded in a voice that left no room for argument.

The guards dropped their guns and knives. Kaynan and Jet gathered the weapons, then forced the guards to leave through the door by the cage. Gem walked up the stairs, her eyes on Nora's father. I helped Nora to her feet, then stumbled and caught myself against the crate.

Nora put a hand on my shoulder, her eyes concerned. "I should be the one helping you," she said in a voice that trembled.

I shook my head. "Seeing you safe is all the help I need."

Jaze pushed Rob in front of him and we walked slowly up the stairs. Dizziness from the crowbar blow to the back of my head kept my steps measured, but it faded as we left the basement. By the time we reached the yard, I felt stronger. Nora touched the back of my hair and when her hand came away bloody, she tried to make me sit down.

"It's alright," I reassured her. "It's already healing."

Jaze pushed Rob toward one of the Hunters' vehicles, then paused. "Is there anything you want to say to your daughter before you leave?"

I felt Nora tense, but she stood firm and waited for his response.

Rob glared from me to his daughter, such hatred and vehemence in his eyes that I wanted to tear them from his face so that no one would look at Nora like that again. Rob spoke in a dark, angry voice, "I never dreamed you would follow in your mother's footsteps, but what should I have expected with werewolf blood in your veins?"

Surprise showed on Nora's face, but she pushed it down. "You didn't have to do this," she said. There was a pleading tone to her voice as if she asked a question, begging her father to show some shred of humanity to redeem himself.

"You don't understand," her father replied. His eyes held hers, asking her to listen. He glanced at me and his gaze narrowed. "The werewolves are a scourge to be wiped from the earth. They taint the bloodlines and they'll turn us all into animals."

"You don't need werewolf blood to be an animal," Nora replied quietly.

Hurt touched her father's eyes and quickly turned to rage. He broke free of Jaze's grasp and dove at me. Jet and Kaynan caught his arms before he took two steps. I stood in front of Nora to shield her from him. "You brainwashed her," he shouted, his eyes rolling in anger.

I shook my head. "I helped her see the truth."

He sputtered. "The truth? The truth is that you're more animal than human. You can't be trusted. You're a savage beast."

Nora stepped from behind me. "Father?" When he

looked at her, she took a calming breath. "I love Vance with all of my heart. I'm sorry your life is so twisted by hatred, and I'll live trying to make up for the damage you've done." She dropped her eyes. "I love you, but I can't stand to be near you anymore after what you've done."

"You're tainted by the beast," he replied, his tone so ugly I wanted to hit him for even talking to her. Jet and Kaynan dragged him back toward the truck. "You're no daughter of mine," he called, raising his voice. "Enjoy having puppies with that animal you call a boyfriend."

Tears sparkled in her eyes, then trailed slowly down her cheeks. She turned her head into my shoulder as her father was lifted into the truck and the door shut behind him.

I put my arms around her and the tension eased from my muscles. I took a deep breath and glanced up at the stars that sparkled in the sky. They winked down on us like tiny gems, reminding me of the grandeur of the world and the miracle that we still lived despite the odds we had faced. The light of the partial moon bathed us in a midnight glow that cast the trees as gray sentries guarding us against the shadows of night.

The moonlight felt gentler, the brush of the breeze weaving through the leaves was softer, and the chirp of crickets hiding in the shadows sounded sweeter. All was right in the world now that Nora was back in my arms. Her scent of vanilla and sunflowers tangled around me and I took a deep breath of it, reluctant to let it out again.

She tipped her head up and her green eyes met mine. The sadness, acceptance, and pain in them stole whatever remained of my heart. "What happens now?" she asked softly.

I leaned down and kissed her on the lips, my fingers entwining gently in her long back hair as she moved a hand to my neck, pulling me closer. I closed my eyes and let her surround me and complete me, covering the pain and torment and chasing away the fears that had filled every day she had been gone. When we parted, I smiled, my eyes gazing into hers. "I don't know," I admitted. Laugh lines touched the corners of her eyes and I continued, "But whatever it is, we face it together."

She touched my face with her hand; her gentle fingers ran along my jaw and sent a shiver up my spine. She smiled and leaned against my chest. I wrapped her in my arms, vowing to never let her go again.

I glanced up and found the others watching us. Gem caught my attention first. She crossed the grass toward us and a pang of regret ran through my bones at the sorrow and realization on her face. My heart ached at the loss in her eyes and for causing her additional pain. She was such a strong, amazing person, and she had earned the right to be happy. I dreaded what she would say, but I deserved to bear the brunt of her pain.

Her eyebrows pulled together and the pixie grin that always danced on her face was sorely absent. She reached up a hand and set it softly on my arm. "I'm happy for you," she said. Her eyes brimmed with tears, but her smile returned and she hugged us both. "I'm so happy for you."

I covered her hand with my own, dwarfing her fingers. She nodded once and stepped back to the others. I felt a small tug in my heart at her distance, but knew it was for the best. The gratitude that flooded through me at everything Gem had done and all she represented made me hold Nora even closer.

My gaze moved to Jaze and he gave a small nod, a look of approval on his face. His words echoed in my head. I took a breath and spoke them quietly to Nora. "You are my night and day, my moon, my stars, and every driving force that keeps my lungs filling up with air and my heart beating to drive blood through my body. Without you, I am not me." I swallowed down the lump that tightened my throat. "You make me more because I am with you. You complete me, and you bring out who I really am." Nora's face turned up to me and fresh tears sparkled in her eyes, but they were symbols of joy instead of sorrow. I smiled through my own tears. "It won't matter where our path takes us as long as we walk it together."

She nodded, her face bathed in moonlight. "I can go anywhere with you now."

I looked down at her and asked, "What do you mean?"

She turned her head slightly and her green eyes glinted golden in the moonlight. "Let me show you," she said softly.

Everyone watched in silence as she stepped back into the house. A faint scent brushed the fabric of my shirt where she had touched me. My heart stirred and I looked up to see a graceful cream colored wolf step onto the porch.

"Whoa," someone whispered behind me.

I glanced at Jaze and saw the smile on his face. "Who knows what love can do," he said softly, his eyes on Nora.

She crossed the lawn to me and I fell to my knees. Tears trickled down my cheeks and she licked them away. I took off my shirt and phased in the basking moonlight. I turned back to the others and Nora stood at my shoulder. Though I was huge and hulking beside her lithe form, I no longer felt like a bear or an uncontrollable beast. I was a protector, a leader, and for the first time in my life, I was complete and stronger because of the gentleness of the one standing next to me.

We crossed the lawn and entered the twilight darkness of the trees beyond. The world around us fell away. We were complete, more together than we were apart, and we had rescued each other from the unthinkable. She was mine and I vowed to never let her go. My heart was whole, and for the first time in my life, I was truly ready to live.

CHEREE ALSOP

## About the Author

Cheree Alsop is the mother of a beautiful, talented daughter and two amazing twin sons who fill every day with light and laughter. She married her best friend, Michael, who changes lives each day in his Chiropractic clinic. Cheree is currently working as a free-lance writer and mother. She enjoys reading, riding her Ninja motorcycle on warm nights, and rocking her twins while planning her next book. She is also an aspiring drummer and bass player for her husband's garage band.

Cheree and Michael live in Utah where they rock out, enjoy the outdoors, plan great adventures, and never stop dreaming.

Printed in Great Britain
by Amazon.co.uk, Ltd.,
Marston Gate.